"Sandstorms can last for minutes or days."

The wind was a living force smashing against the Land Rover. Dust particles penetrated every crack and crevice, and Elyn felt panic bubbling within her. "I can't stay in here," she gasped. "There's no air left!"

As she hurled herself against the door, Alex seized her and pressed her against his chest. "You must stay inside," he said sharply.

Unconsciously, like a child, Elyn nestled closer, and in a blinding flash of clarity she realized he was going to kiss her. And with that realization came despair.

His kisses on her eyes, cheeks and throat branded her skin. But his kisses meant nothing—how could they when she meant nothing? It was just a way to control her hysterical outburst without slapping her face.

WELCOME
TO THE WONDERFUL WORLD
OF *Harlequin Romances*

Interesting, informative and entertaining,
each Harlequin Romance portrays an appealing
and original love story. With a varied array
of settings, we may lure you on an African safari,
to a quaint Welsh village, or an exotic Riviera
location—anywhere and everywhere that adventurous
men and women fall in love.

As publishers of Harlequin Romances, we're
extremely proud of our books. Since 1949,
Harlequin Enterprises has built its publishing
reputation on the solid base of quality and
originality. Our stories are the most popular
paperback romances sold in North America; every
month, six new titles are released and sold at
nearly every book-selling store in Canada and the
United States.

A free catalog listing all Harlequin Romances
can be yours by writing to the

HARLEQUIN READER SERVICE,
(In the U.S.) P.O. Box 52040, Phoenix, AZ 85072-2040
(In Canada) P.O. Box 2800, Postal Station A
5170 Yonge Street, Willowdale, Ont. M2N 5T5

We sincerely hope you enjoy reading
this Harlequin Romance.

Yours truly,

THE PUBLISHERS
Harlequin Romances

Desert Flower

Dana James

Harlequin Books

TORONTO • NEW YORK • LONDON
AMSTERDAM • PARIS • SYDNEY • HAMBURG
STOCKHOLM • ATHENS • TOKYO • MILAN

Original hardcover edition published in 1983
by Mills & Boon Limited

ISBN 0-373-02632-3

Harlequin Romance first edition July 1984

CHAPTER ONE

Cairo International Airport was a hive of noise and activity. As Elyn entered the terminal after leaving the comparative quiet of the British Airways 747 jet, she felt a mild surge of panic as she was swept up by a moving current of bodies. Bodies whose colours ranged from white to ebony, and included every shade in between.

Blue uniforms festooned with gold braid, and khaki uniforms with strange insignia rubbed shoulders with white djellabas and mud-coloured burnouses. Brilliantly-patterned saris floated like gaudy butterflies among the pastel cotton dresses and lightweight suits in the bustling concourse.

The dark-eyed scrutiny of the Egyptian customs officers, with revolvers at their waists, and the armed guards outside passport control jolted Elyn with the sudden realisation that this was indeed a foreign country.

She fought her way through the crush to a tall pillar near the exit doors. She dropped her case by her feet and leaned thankfully against the pillar. There were so many people. It was as though the eight million population which made Cairo the largest city in Africa, were all crammed into the airport. They eddied around her like a tide. The volume of noise was deafening. No-one seemed to speak in anything softer than a shout.

Elyn glanced at her watch. It was almost 7.30 pm local time, that made it 5.30 in England. Teatime. A momentary pang of homesickness stabbed her. Aunt Connie would have the kettle on and the delicious scent of home-made cake and scones and perhaps a fruit tart, would waft through from the kitchen.

Her father would emerge from the study, where he spent every waking minute that he wasn't at the Lab, working on his notes. His glasses would be pushed up on his forehead and his hair rumpled and untidy from his habit of scratching his head when pondering a difficult problem concerning his research. Elyn loved to join them when she wasn't on duty. She gave herself a mental shake. This was no way to approach the exciting challenge that awaited her. She must look forward, not back. She must stop thinking of her own feelings and concentrate on the people she hoped would benefit from her being here.

Elyn glanced at her watch again. Where was Dr Davidson? The letter had said he would meet her inside the airport building, but hadn't specified exactly where. Would he ever find her in this crowd?

Elyn shivered and pulled her thin cardigan around her. She had left London basking in the unexpected warmth of an Indian summer. Here air-conditioning moderated the extreme heat of the day-time temperature, and cooled the warm, stale air exhausted by hundreds of milling people. But Elyn was cold and, she had to admit, rather apprehensive.

St Mary's Hospital could have been on another planet and Elyn was assailed by doubts. Had the two years she had spent there as a junior doctor been adequate preparation for the job she had taken on?

A harassed young man with sandy hair sticking out in all directions caught his foot against her suitcase and stumbled. He was wearing a checked shirt and faded jeans, both covered in a layer of dust, some of which he shed over Elyn as he lurched forward.

Elyn started to apologise, but the young man, without bothering to look at her, muttered something and pushed past, fighting against the crowd, obviously in a great hurry.

Elyn shrank back against the pillar, hugging her ancient leather shoulder bag close to her.

It had been a present from Mike, her fiancé. Ex-fiancé she corrected herself. She could think about him now and it didn't hurt. It was nearly three months since that fateful Tuesday evening. Aunt Connie had been out and her father had been deeply immersed in his notes in the study when the doorbell had rung. Elyn remembered looking at her watch; nine-thirty, late for visitors.

She had been surprised and thrilled to see Mike. They had a date for the weekend and Elyn had not expected to see or hear from him before then.

In fact, seeing him standing there reminded her how little they'd actually been together that month.

Mike had been even busier than usual with his job, which involved quite a bit of travelling, and she had had a couple of spells of extra duty, covering for colleagues on holiday.

Elyn flung her arms around Mike in delighted welcome, but instead of kissing her and holding her close, he freed himself with almost indecent haste and before she had a chance to realise that something was wrong, blurted out that it was all over between them, he'd fallen in love with someone else. Someone who was gay and frivolous and fun to be with.

Totally unprepared for this bombshell, Elyn had been shocked and bewildered. 'Do you mean I'm none of those things, then?' she'd asked in a daze.

Mike had shaken his head impatiently. 'You're too dedicated, Elyn. You couldn't satisfy your need to help the human race by just being a nurse, you had to go one better and be a doctor.'

Elyn could hardly believe her ears. 'But Mike, you knew that when we met and we've been engaged for over two years.'

Elyn recalled vividly Mike's obvious pride when he'd introduced her to his friends. 'This is Elyn, my fiancée,' he'd say, 'she's a doctor!'

Elyn herself had sometimes found his pride in her job a slight embarrassment, not to mention it being a real problem when people started asking for medical advice or complaining about the treatment they were receiving from their own GP or local hospital.

'You never told me you felt like that about my work,'

Elyn said, trying desperately to understand. 'I thought you realised it was more than just a nine-to-five job. Like your own. Your company sends you all over the world, sometimes at only a few hours' notice. I've always accepted that.'

'Yes,' Mike countered swiftly, 'and many's the time you could have come with me, but you were always on duty or on call or studying.'

'But—' Elyn began.

'It's no good, Elyn,' Mike interrupted, 'I want a wife who will fit into *my* life, who'll devote herself entirely to me, not someone I have to make an appointment with.'

Elyn bit her lip to try and stop it trembling. 'Well,' she said quietly, 'in that case, I don't suppose there's anything more to be said.' Twisting the diamond solitaire from her finger she held it out to him.

'You can keep it if you like,' he muttered uncomfortably.

Elyn quickly shook her head. 'Oh no. It wasn't just a piece of jewellery, it was a symbol of—' she swallowed the lump in her throat, 'anyway, the things it stood for no longer exist, so I think you should have it back.'

Mike shrugged and slipped the ring into his pocket. He moved uncomfortably from one foot to the other. 'Well, I'd better be off then. Lots to do. We're off to America tomorrow—' he broke off, shame-faced. 'Look, I didn't mean—'

Gathering the remnants of her pride, Elyn drew herself up. 'That's all right, Mike. Have a good trip,' she said quietly, opening the door for him to leave, 'goodbye.'

He paused on the threshold. 'We can still be friends, can't we?' he said eagerly, obviously relieved that an unpleasant task had been accomplished so easily. A hopeful smile curved his lips. Those lips that only days before had so expertly kissed her, causing her heart to thud in her breast and a thrill of desire like summer lightning. While he had been kissing her had he been thinking of his new love?

'Goodbye, Mike,' Elyn repeated and closed the door softly but firmly. Then, leaning against it she had let the tears come. Tears of sadness and loss, tears of anger at the way he'd behaved behind her back and tears of bewilderment and doubt.

Had her ambition destroyed her femininity? Was she wrong to want to be a doctor? Was she really no fun to be with, a dried-up, over-serious spinster at twenty-five?

Elyn fingered the smooth leather flap of her bag and pushed the remembered doubts aside. She realised now that she and Mike had wanted different things from life and from each other. Despite his lip-service to her achievements, he would have hated having a wife with a career of her own. He would have seen it as a threat to his ego and a criticism of his status as the breadwinner.

Elyn did not feel a threat to anyone, nor was she interested in status. She only knew that she loved the challenge and demands of her work and was not ready to give it up to stay at home to look after someone who was not often there anyway.

Still, standing here in Cairo airport, waiting for the senior medical officer in charge of a small clinic to whisk her off into the desert, was a far cry from the Casualty Department at St Mary's!

Elyn's mouth curved in a small smile as she looked about her. Here she was at last, after weeks of planning, only a few miles from immense trackless desert wastes, yet surrounded by more people than she had ever seen in her life.

Her moment of reflection was rudely interrupted by the shock of seeing a wiry, olive-skinned Arab in a dirt-stained djellaba grasp the handle of her brand-new leather suitcase.

Unable in the shock of the moment to remember a word of her painfully learned Arabic, Elyn grabbed at the man's arm.

'Stop. Put that down. You've made a mistake. That case is mine.' Her voice was barely audible even to her own ears above the din going on around them. The Arab tugged his arm free, nodding his head rapidly. The harsh gutteral sounds of his native tongue rattling from his mouth.

'Please let go.' Elyn heard the panic in her voice and tried desperately to control it. She was a stranger in a strange land, to show fear would invite disaster. But what was she to do? The Arab still had hold of her case and though she had seized the sleeve of his grubby cotton garment, he was pushing and struggling through the crowd in an effort to reach the exit, and she was being pulled along with him.

Fear clutched with cold fingers at Elyn's heart. She looked around frantically. Wouldn't someone help her? But there was so much noise and pushing and shoving going on, unless she screamed at the top of her lungs and really created an uproar, no-one was going to notice what was happening.

The thought of being the centre of attention and for such a reason made Elyn go hot and cold. Her natural shyness shrank from such an exhibition, yet common sense dictated that if she didn't do something quickly, the Arab would have parted her from her suitcase and she would be stranded with nothing but her shoulder bag and the clothes she was wearing.

Elyn took a deep breath. 'Let go of my case at once or I'll call the police,' she shouted, her voice wavering.

'That won't be necessary,' a deep voice announced curtly, and a tanned muscular arm shot past her ear and landed on the Arab's shoulder. The Arab turned, his eyes wide with what Elyn took to be feigned surprise.

In the same deep tones the stranger spoke a few crisp sentences, the throat-tearing sounds flowing swiftly and effortlessly from his lips. The Arab dropped the case as though it had suddenly become red-hot. He shrugged elaborately, his shoulders rising so high that his head nearly disappeared between them. With palms upturned and an ingratiating smile revealing stained and blackened teeth, still jabbering, he backed away into the crowd and was immediately swallowed up.

Elyn retrieved her case, gripping the handle tightly. Her knees felt distinctly wobbly. Fighting to recover her composure, she kept her eyes lowered as she turned to her rescuer.

'Thank you so much. It really was very kind—' her voice was breathless with relief.

'It was nothing,' the stranger dismissed her gratitude abruptly. 'The man has an arrangement with one of the taxi drivers outside. He gets a tip for every customer he brings the cabbie.' The stranger's voice was terse, and though hardly raised, penetrated the babble on all sides without effort. Its brusqueness implied that anyone but her would have realised what was happening.

Elyn looked up quickly, a crimson blush staining her cheeks, a tremulous smile of apology on her lips.

'I thought he was trying to steal my case.'

The eyes that looked down into hers were green with strange gold flecks, and the expression in them was anything but friendly.

Above the straight brows drawn together in a frown, his dark hair was brushed back in unruly waves from his deep forehead. The cold hard lines of his nose and jaw looked as though they'd been hewn from granite.

He was like a rock. The tide of people broke and swirled about him, never jostling or touching him. It was as if they sensed an aloneness that kept them, despite the crowded conditions, at a slight distance.

'He was probably trying to earn enough to buy food for his family tonight,' the stranger said impatiently. 'Are you alone?'

Elyn flinched at the question. She suddenly felt like a little girl again, with her Aunt Connie's warnings about strangers ringing in her ears.

As if reading her thoughts, the stranger exploded, 'For heaven's sake, I'm not trying to pick you up, I have more important things to do. Now, are you alone?'

'I'm—I'm being met,' Elyn answered hastily.

'Then hurry up and find whoever is meeting you. Get the Arrivals Desk to page them on the tannoy,' he ordered. 'Hanging about alone in a place like this is just asking for trouble, and next time it might not be so easily dealt with.'

Elyn flushed deeply. He was treating her like some silly schoolgirl. She turned her anger to Dr Davidson. Why hadn't he met her as he'd promised? If he had, this whole embarrassing incident would not have occurred and she would not have had to put up with a lecture from a bad-tempered, self-opinionated bully.

'Thank you for your concern,' Elyn returned, managing to inject cool politeness into her voice, though her heart was thumping furiously and she could feel her cheeks burning, 'actually, I'm quite capable of looking after myself.'

The stranger's lips twitched, so quickly that Elyn thought she must have imagined it. It couldn't possibly have been a smile. But the twitch had brought a glimmer of warmth to his steely gaze.

Just then a stunningly beautiful woman slipped a slender beringed hand through his arm. Her midnight hair was piled high in a glossy coil and her olive skin and huge dark eyes proclaimed her middle-eastern origin.

'Not another lame duck, Alex,' she exclaimed, her husky voice with its lightly-accented English assuming pained tones. Her glance flickered in rapid assessment over Elyn's slender figure, her blue cotton dress, creased from the long flight, her heart-shaped face which was bare of make-up, and her boyish cropped hair.

The hint of amusement went out of the stranger's eyes as though a shutter had slammed down. Elyn flushed once more. So that was their opinion of her, a lame duck.

Unconsciously she raised one arm and ran her fingers through her gleaming chestnut curls. She still wasn't used to her new hairstyle. Aunt Connie had advised her to have her almost waist-length hair cut short.

'If you are determined to go to this godforsaken place, you'll find it much easier to manage. Just think of the heat, and there might not be much water,' she had warned. 'Heaven only knows what passengers you might end up carrying in that lot.' Her horrified expression had made Elyn laugh, but there had been a lot of sense in her advice.

So Elyn had fitted the appointment into her busy schedule and had emerged somewhat lightheaded and quite surprised by the alteration in her appearance.

Her eyes, accentuated by the soft natural curls that framed her face, suddenly seemed much larger and had deepened from cornflower to sapphire. Her cheekbones seemed more prominent and her chin smaller. It had been almost like looking at a stranger.

As the woman's musky, sophisticated perfume pervaded Elyn's nostrils she was suddenly uncomfortably aware of her own travel-stained appearance. Her bare legs and sandalled feet were dusty and she was sure her nose was shining.

The other woman, cool and chic in a bronze linen trouser suit, her cursory inspection complete, turned her gaze away. Elyn felt herself dismissed as surely as if a wall had appeared between herself and the elegant Egyptian.

'Come, Alex,' she murmured, 'go and sign your beastly papers, then let's go out to dinner. I'll fly you back tomorrow instead.' She gazed meltingly up at him from kohl-lined eyes fringed with sooty lashes.

'I think not, Samina. I don't want to be away longer than necessary.'

He sounds tired, no not just tired, he sounds exhausted, Elyn thought with surprise. Not that it was any of her business of course. Yet she could not resist a quick glance up at him. To her chagrin his own cool green gaze met hers.

'I hate flying at night, darling,' Samina purred throatily. 'It makes me nervous!'

Elyn could not imagine anyone more totally self-possessed than the immaculately clad and flawlessly made-up woman before her. Still, perhaps that calm exterior was just a mask hiding the fear underneath.

Elyn had felt her own heart pound and her palms dampen as the huge jet had shuddered under the thrust of its mighty engines screaming to full power before the plane rolled slowly then faster and faster down the runway, eventually lifting off into the late September sunshine.

But unless Elyn had misheard, this woman was actually a pilot, not a passenger. Surely pilots didn't get nervous?

'The three flights you insisted on making this month alone should have taken the edge off your nerves,' he replied pleasantly, but gave her no answering smile. 'However, if you prefer, I can hire a jeep.'

'Oh Alex, there's no need for that,' Samina pouted, petulance darkening her beautiful face. 'I said I'd fly you back, though why you have to go tonight I can't imagine. Anyone else would wait until morning. Honestly, Alex, your preoccupation with work is making you positively anti-social.'

Elyn began to feel distinctly uncomfortable. Yet she could not deny the pang of sympathy she felt for the tall dark stranger. Hadn't Mike accused her of just the same thing?

But their personal differences were none of her concern. Alex obviously thought the same for as he turned from the Egyptian to her Elyn could sense his barely concealed impatience.

'Go to the International Arrivals Desk and stay there until whoever is meeting you turns up. English may be a common language here, but you are not in England now, don't forget that.'

On those parting words he turned away and, placing a none too gentle arm beneath Samina's elbow, he began to move with her through the crowd. His tall figure, clad in khaki bush shirt and trousers, was visible for some moments above the jostling heads.

'Yes, sir, right away, sir,' Elyn murmured angrily. Who did he think he was, ordering her about like that. Was he trying to frighten her? She certainly didn't need reminding that she was in a foreign country. For a moment her doubts flooded back. Had she really done a wise thing coming here? Should she have stayed on at St Mary's? Did she have the courage to remain in this alien place, which was not as alien as the desert that awaited her?

Grubby fingers tugging at her sleeve, an ingratiating smile accompanied by a harsh flood of Arabic, had Elyn clutching her suitcase, grabbing her shoulder bag tightly and pushing hurriedly through the crowd to the Arrivals Desk.

She approached the clerk and, slipping in through a momentary gap, explained what had happened. The clerk spoke good English and was sympathetic. He scribbled down the names and switched on a microphone, drawing it towards him.

'Would the representative of Khalifa Clinic please come to the International Arrivals Desk. Khalifa Clinic, your passenger is waiting.' The message echoed metallically through the hall.

Elyn wondered why the clerk had not given their names then it dawned on her. She did not know what Dr Davidson looked like. If the clerk had said that Miss Scott was waiting, any man could have come up and said he was there to meet her, and if she did not think of checking his credentials, she could have left the comparative safety of the building and been in serious trouble before realising it. But no-one except her would know the name of the person she was meeting. It was a safety check.

The clerks were obviously trained to help prevent such incidents occurring. Elyn made a silent apology to the tall stranger, Alex whoever-he-was. She was only just beginning to realise how vulnerable she was. Despite all the warnings, it hadn't really sunk in that anything could happen to her.

Elyn scanned the crowd with anxious eyes. People jostling round the desk were forced apart by the sandy-haired young man who earlier had stumbled over her case. He erupted out of the crowd and waved to attract the clerk's attention.

'I'm Tim Preston,' he called, showing his open passport to the clerk over the heads of the people, 'I'm here to collect Dr Scott, Dr Davidson's passenger for Khalifa.'

The clerk, busy with several enquiries, gestured, pointing towards Elyn, who had seen the exchange. She smiled with relief, stepped forward. But his gaze swept over and past her, still searching. A frown drew his brows together and with muttered exasperation he turned back to the desk and tried to attract the clerk's attention once more.

Realising something was wrong, Elyn moved forward and touched Tim Preston's arm. He swung round. 'Yes, what is it?' he said, impatiently.

Elyn was taken aback by his attitude. What was it about this place that caused people to be so appallingly rude, she wondered. She hoped it wasn't going to be like this with everyone she met.

Colouring pinkly under the young man's stare, Elyn introduced herself.

'I'm the person you're here to meet. I asked the clerk to page Dr Davidson,' she explained, 'we somehow missed each other—'

'But you can't be,' he interrupted, disbelief replacing his impatient frown. He looked her up and down. 'I'm supposed to be meeting a chap called Scott.'

'My name *is* Scott,' Elyn replied, 'I'm Dr Elyn Scott.' She opened her handbag, 'look, my passport and visa and the letter from the World Health Organisation approving my application to join Dr Davidson's clinic at Khalifa.'

Tim Preston glanced at the documents, then gave a guffaw of laughter. 'Davidson thought your name was Glyn, he's expecting a man. His face will be a picture when he sets eyes on you. He swore he'd never work with another female after the last disaster WHO sent out.'

Elyn's immediate reaction was anger. How dare he refer to her even by implication as a disaster. Suddenly it was very important for her to reach the oasis and the settlement with its small clinic and prove that not only was she equal to the work, but that the fact that she was a woman made no difference to her capability. Whatever problems Dr Davidson had experienced with his last assistant, they were nothing to do with her.

Straightening her back and lifting her chin, Elyn met Tim Preston's amused stare. 'Obviously there has been a misunderstanding, and equally obviously I'm not a man. But as I was engaged on the strength of my qualifications I don't see that it matters. Where is Dr Davidson anyway?'

Tim Preston threw up his hands in mock surrender. 'He sends his apologies but he had some problems over a special consignment of drugs from Switzerland. The authorities wouldn't release them without his signature,' he grimaced, 'affixed in person in triplicate on all the relevant forms. He also had some meetings to attend, though I know he hates being away from the clinic, even for a day. I had to come down to collect some cases of special seeds which had gone astray and missed the internal flight, so he asked me to deputise. A duty more pleasurable than I anticipated,' he smiled warmly at Elyn. 'You sure you want to go on with this? Alex Davidson will give you a hard time.'

Elyn nodded quickly. 'I came out to do a job, Mr Preston, I'm not one to give up easily.'

'No,' he shook his head slowly, 'I guess you're not.' Picking up her suitcase he pushed his way through the thronging mass of people. Elyn was struggling to keep up with him when it hit her like a blow. Alex, Tim had called Dr Davidson Alex!

Elyn had a vivid mental picture of the tall dark man who had come to her rescue; it couldn't be him, it couldn't be. There must be dozens of Europeans in Cairo called Alex. It wasn't such an uncommon name.

Besides, why should he have been in the airport? The consignment—'sign your beastly forms', Samina had said. Elyn swallowed hard.

If by some awful quirk of fate Dr Davidson and the cold-eyed contemptuous stranger were one and the same, there was absolutely nothing she could do about it. All the wishing in the world wouldn't erase that embarrassing encounter. She would simply have to hope that her dedication to dealing with any task he might set her would put it out of his mind, though judging by what Tim had said, she was going to have to work doubly hard to achieve that.

Sitting in the dust-caked Land Rover with Elyn's suit-case balanced on top of wooden crates and bulging sacks, Tim rested both hands on the steering wheel and turned to her.

'Do you have any idea of the conditions you'll be facing? It will be nothing like you're used to. Khalifa is just a small settlement, very rough and ready. There's no proper air-conditioning, even in the clinic. The days are stifling hot and the nights bitterly cold, there's dirt, dust and disease.'

Elyn gave him a small smile, but her fingers gripped her bag tightly as she struggled to control the upheaval of emotions within her.

'It's true I have not lived or worked in the desert before, Mr Preston, but I've read a lot about it in preparation. I wouldn't have applied for the job if I didn't think I could live with the hardships and discomforts and still work efficiently.'

Even to her own ears Elyn sounded defensive, but she couldn't help herself. He wouldn't be talking like that if she were a man.

'Hey, no need for all this formality, call me Tim, everybody does. OK if I call you Elyn?' he grinned. Elyn suddenly felt better. She relaxed, realising as she did so how uptight she'd been.

'All right, Tim,' she smiled back. 'Do you work at the clinic?' she asked curiously as he started the engine and threaded the Land Rover out of the carpark onto the main road.

He shook his head, 'No, my territory is south of the settlement, between Khalifa and Kharga oasis. I'm an agronomist.'

'That's something to do with rural economy, or agriculture, isn't it?' Elyn asked as they roared down wide-paved avenues lined with tall palms and neon street lights, fine examples of civil engineering in a modern metropolis. Elyn was torn between trying to see something of the city through the darkness and listening to Tim.

He nodded. 'We're part of the same social plan that includes your clinic. A pattern of new water wells have been sunk between Kharga and Khalifa following the discovery of a deep underground reservoir. The government is desperate to stop the oasis-dwellers migrating to the Nile valley which is already overcrowded and over-cultivated. The south side of the Kharga oasis is being threatened by a huge barchan dune field.'

'Just a sec, Tim,' Elyn interrupted, 'sorry, but what's a barchan dune?'

'It's a crescent-shaped sand dune,' he explained, 'formed when sand is blown against something in its way, a rock or a bush. The sand piles up behind it as the dune grows, sand grains are swept round the edges forming horns that point down-wind.'

'I see,' Elyn nodded, 'do go on.'

'Sure I'm not boring you?' Tim glanced at her, then gave his attention to the road. 'Like you, I'm keen on my job.'

'Not at all,' Elyn shook her head, 'it's fascinating.'

'Well, as I said, with the south side being threatened, we must extend northwards and develop as much land as possible including Khalifa, which is only a small settlement at the moment.'

'Why was the clinic built at Khalifa?' Elyn asked. 'According to my map, it's out in the middle of nowhere.'

Tim swung the wheel, turning off the main road into a series of narrow winding streets. 'Kharga already has a small hospital and I think Khalifa is a sort of spearhead of the new development,' he replied, 'but Alex Davidson is the best person to ask about that.'

'Yes, of course,' Elyn felt herself shrink from asking Alex Davidson anything at all, the memory of his cutting impatience was all too vivid. 'How much land is going to be involved in the plan?'

'We're working on about two thousand acres at the moment,' Tim answered, 'but we'll be increasing that rapidly as new wells are sunk.'

Elyn was impressed. 'How many of you are there?' she asked.

'The whole adult population of the oasis,' Tim laughed. 'But if you mean the team organising it, there are nine of us. The project director is an Egyptian, Mr Mahmoud El-Sheikh, then there's Bill Jennings and myself, we're both specialists in desert reclamation, and assisting us with actually instructing the fellaheen in intensive production methods and crop rotation, we've six Egyptians.'

'Hey, look out of the window.' Tim slowed down.

Elyn did as she was told and saw that they were crawling through a dusty souk, where rickety stalls and tiny shops displayed goods of every description. Fruit and vegetables, carpets, pottery, leather, brass and fabrics of every hue and texture, their vivid colours reflected in the shiny flickering lamps that hung from every upright post, giving the place a festive, carnival atmosphere.

Mouthwatering smells of cooking meat, spices and roasting coffee blended in the cold night air, and Elyn could hardly contain her excitement.

'Oh, isn't it lovely. It's even better than I imagined, it's so—'

'Romantic?' Tim offered, grinning.

Elyn blushed. 'I was only going to say that it's so thrilling when reality lives up to one's dream.'

'For goodness' sake don't let Alex hear you say something like that, a woman with fairytale notions about the mysterious East is the last thing he needs, especially after the last one.'

'That's unfair and uncalled for,' Elyn cried, stung by his remark. 'I told you I'd read a lot about Egypt. Naturally I'd formed ideas about aspects of life here. Seeing the souk, it was just as I'd pictured it, but that doesn't mean I'm unaware of the poverty and squalor that exist behind the doors and beaded curtains, or the high death rate amongst children, or deformity and disease that could probably be prevented by elementary medical aid and lessons in hygiene.'

'Whoops, someone's touchy,' Tim said lightly. 'Still, I suppose you're tired.'

'Yes, I am rather,' Elyn admitted. 'Sorry I snapped. Are we going all the way to Khalifa tonight?'

She tried vainly to keep the apprehension out of her voice. The thought of several more hours in the Land Rover, on top of the flight and the incident at the airport, was more than she cared to contemplate.

To her intense relief, Tim shook his head. 'No, it's not safe to travel in the desert at night, distances are distorted. Apart from that we have a drive of about 200 miles to Şuhag before we turn off onto the desert road, and I certainly don't feel like tackling that without a good night's sleep.'

Elyn nodded thankfully. She allowed herself to contemplate a hot bath complete with bath crystals and scented soap. If it was to be the last bath she'd have for some time, as there would certainly be only showers at the clinic, then she was going to revel in it. Then something to eat, followed by a soft bed and hours of blissful sleep, and she would be ready to face whatever this strange country of violent contrasts might hold for her, even Dr Alex Davidson.

They left the souk behind and were now threading their way through a grid plan of low apartment blocks, built, Tim explained, to house the workers in the huge industrial plants which were part of the city's complex economy.

Tim glanced at Elyn. 'What made you decide to come out here?' he asked curiously.

'Several things,' Elyn said slowly. 'I felt the need for a change, and it was a great opportunity to gain practical experience in treatment of sub-tropical diseases.'

'What about your family? How did they take it? Not to mention your boyfriend.'

Elyn smothered a smile at Tim's rather obvious probing. 'Dad gave the sort of astonished grunt he usually reserves for election results, then told me the experience would stand me in good stead for a consultancy.'

'Your father's in medicine, too, is he?'

'In a way. Actually he's a bio-chemist,' Elyn replied. 'I think he was a bit disappointed that I took up practical medicine instead of following him into research. Being an only child, I suppose he had hoped that I'd continue his work.'

'That's quite a responsibility for—' he broke off.

'A girl?' Elyn supplied with a quizzical smile.

'I was going to say for an only child,' Tim corrected her, grinning. 'Anyway, what was your mother's reaction?'

'My mother died when I was two, a road accident,' Elyn said briefly, her smile fading. There was a moment of silence. Then with a determined brightness she went on. 'But Aunt Connie, my father's elder sister, came to live with us. She'd been a widow for several years and had no children of her own. She gave me as much love as any mother could have done. When I told her I'd been accepted for the clinic job, her main concerns were that I had my hair cut and that I had six months' supply of a reliable laxative. Aunt Connie blames all the world's troubles on "irregularity".' Elyn smiled fondly, thinking of her aunt.

Tim's eyes swivelled towards her. Moonlight beamed into the Land Rover, its cold clarity revealing Elyn's elfin features as she gazed ahead through the windscreen at the endless road.

'It's pretty,' Tim remarked.

'What is?' Elyn, miles away, was startled.

'Your hair.'

Elyn felt colour warm her cheeks. She wasn't used to compliments, and was uncertain of how to handle them. But Tim didn't wait for her reaction. 'Now tell me what your boyfriend thought of this expedition,' Tim demanded, 'and don't expect me to believe he didn't object.'

'He wasn't in a position to object,' Elyn said lightly, 'because he didn't know.'

'Didn't you tell him, then?' Tim sounded faintly shocked.

'No—I didn't mean—you don't understand, our engagement was broken off before I applied for the clinic post,' Elyn said quickly, looking down at her clasped hands, bare of rings, then staring out of the window.

'Aaah,' Tim invested the sound with a wealth of meaning.

As the Land Rover roared on, both lapsed into silence, each involved in their own thoughts.

Then, without warning Tim spun the wheel and the Land Rover turned off the road into a dusty yard fringed with stunted palms. He switched off the engine and the sudden silence was loud in Elyn's ears. 'Where are we?' she asked, craning to look round.

Tim was already climbing out of the Land Rover. He leaned into the back and hauled out a battered overnight bag. 'This is where we spend the night,' he announced.

'Is it an hotel?' Elyn looked out of her window at the two-storey, sand-coloured building. A flickering lamp hung next to the shadowed doorway.

'Of sorts,' was Tim's brief reply. 'It's not the Ritz, but it is clean and the food's good.'

Elyn wondered by what standard Tim Preston judged cleanliness and had a suspicion that it wouldn't be the same as hers.

'Come on then,' he urged, pulling her case out of the Land Rover and dropping it on the ground beside his bag. Elyn climbed out obediently, stretching to ease the stiffness in her limbs. She waited while he locked the Land Rover carefully, checking each handle, then followed him through the shadowed doorway.

The aroma of roast meat and onions and mint tea made her mouth water and she suddenly realised how hungry she was.

Tim was talking to an Arab in a striped djellaba who had a strip of white cloth bound round his head like a turban. The man, whose olive skin was as wrinkled as a walnut, was gesturing and talking in staccato bursts, with much bowing, headshaking and shrugging. Tim appeared to be arguing with him about something, but obviously wasn't getting very far.

Elyn wished they would hurry up so that she could have something to eat. A peep through the bead-curtained doorway on her right showed her that the large main room was crowded. The majority of its occupants were Arab, but she caught sight of two European faces. Dishes rattled, voices murmured in conversation and the hot, savoury smell of food wafted out to her.

Elyn tugged Tim's sleeve. With a final shrug the Arab had turned away and was walking up the narrow staircase.

'Can we go to our rooms now,' Elyn pleaded, 'I'm simply starving, but I'd love a bath first, if you don't mind,' she added.

'I don't mind at all,' he said, with an odd grin, and, picking up her suitcase and his bag, led the way up the stairs.

The Arab proprietor was waiting for them at the top. He led them along a passage and stopped outside a heavy wooden door. Turning the handle he pushed it open and gestured for them to enter, again with much bowing.

Elyn went in first while Tim gave the man a crumpled note from his wallet and received in return a huge iron key. The Arab bowed again and shuffled away down the passage.

To Elyn's surprise the room *was* clean. The carpets on the floor were worn and threadbare, but had been freshly beaten, the floor itself had been swept. The sheets on the twin beds were crisp and white and the blue coverlets had been freshly laundered. Two oil lamps stood on the wooden chest, which though scarred and stained was free of dust. A cracked mirror above the chest reflected the lamplight.

Elyn turned to Tim who was standing just inside the door, watching her.

'Thank you,' she smiled, stretching out her hand for the key, 'it's quite luxurious really. I can manage now if you'll just tell me where the bathroom is.'

'At the end of the passage,' Tim replied, the strange grin still playing round his mouth. 'Our host has gone to clear the tub of spiders, snakes and scorpions and to send for hot water.'

Elyn shuddered, then realised he might be teasing, but on reflection accepted that he was probably telling the truth.

She bit her lip and kept quiet. If he was telling the truth, it was something else about life out here that she'd just have to get used to.

'The key please, Tim?' Elyn repeated, her smile becoming a little strained. She hoped he wasn't going to be difficult.

'Sorry, Elyn,' he gave an apologetic shrug, 'remember I told you at the airport I expected a man? Well, as a concession to your femininity, you can choose which bed you want.'

Elyn stiffened and her eyes opened wide. She stared at him, speechless.

'But, if you've no preference, I'll take the one by the door,' Tim said calmly and, lifting his bag onto the coverlet, opened it and began lifting out shaving gear and pyjamas.

'What do you think you're doing?' Elyn said faintly.

'Stop that at once. I'm not sharing a room with you, it's ridiculous.'

'Not as ridiculous as you spending the night in the Land Rover, but you can if you'd rather,' he replied, and drawing the keys from his trouser pocket he tossed them to her.

Elyn caught them automatically. Tim watched her as she stared at them and bit her lip, her thoughts racing.

'Look,' he explained patiently, 'I booked this room on the way down to Cairo. The place is crowded, you saw that when we came in. I've asked, but there isn't even a broom cupboard to spare. I've had a hectic day, and I've got three hundred miles of hard driving ahead of me tomorrow, I need a decent night's sleep.' He spread his hands and shrugged. 'Now you can take that bed and be comfortable or you can play the virtuous Victorian miss and sleep in the Land Rover. Of course it will be very cold and there might be prowlers about, but it's entirely your choice.'

With that he turned away and resumed his unpacking.

CHAPTER TWO

ELYN was rooted to the spot, her mind in turmoil. Of all the problems she had envisaged, this particular one had never entered her head.

She was hungry and tired, and the thought of sleeping in the cold, cramped Land Rover, visible to any prying eyes, was unbearable. But she had met Tim Preston only a few hours ago and knew almost nothing about him. Was he to be trusted?

As if reading her thoughts, Tim looked round, a clean checked shirt in his hands. 'Look, I didn't plan this. I mean, I didn't know you were a woman—oh, you know what I mean,' he finished in exasperation. 'Honestly, Elyn, I did ask about another room, but—' he shrugged, not bothering to complete the sentence.

Elyn bit her lip and lifted one shoulder in a helpless gesture. 'We'll just have to manage, I suppose.' Bending her head to hide the pinkness in her cheeks she lifted her case onto the second bed and took out the items she needed.

'I'm going to have a bath,' she announced levelly, as if sharing a room at a desert inn with a strange man was nothing out of the ordinary.

Tim nodded and grinned. 'Want me to scrub your back?'

'I can manage,' she said quickly, and hurried out, cheeks burning.

She lay in the ancient tub, letting the warm water wash away her tiredness along with the dust, and emerged fresh and cool. Dressed in a cream Indian cotton blouse and a long, brightly patterned skirt, Elyn slipped her feet into her sandals. She pulled a comb through her chestnut curls, added a touch of lipstick and she was ready. Perhaps makeup out here on the fringe of the desert was

27

a small vanity, but it boosted her morale, and right now her confidence needed all the help it could get. Swinging a mohair shawl around her shoulders, the coral shade reflected in the pattern of her skirt, Elyn collected her toilet-bag, towel and clothes and returned to the bedroom.

Tim opened the door to her knock. He had used the jug and bowl on the stand in the corner to freshen up. His freckled face was free of dust and his hair damp and freshly combed, though it still refused to lie flat. He had put on a clean shirt and had shaken the worst of the dust from his jeans.

'Hey, don't you look pretty?' he said admiringly and pursed his lips in a silent whistle. 'There's no-one else I'd rather be sharing a room with.'

Elyn walked past him. 'Just watch it,' she warned, only half-joking. She replaced her toilet-bag and crumpled clothes in her suitcase and hung her towel over the bottom of the bedstead to dry.

'Lady, I won't take my eyes off you,' Tim promised, his hand over his heart.

Elyn found his flattery and his obvious attraction to her a much needed boost to her ego, which, though she had completely recovered from her broken engagement, was still a little bruised. But she was not ready for another entanglement yet.

She picked up her bag and walked out into the passage. 'Stop teasing,' she begged, and started down the stairs.

'Who's teasing?' Tim followed her, locking the door, then spread his hands in mock innocence.

Elyn paused on the threshold of the dining room. There was no door, but strings of bright beads hung from lintel to floor in a curtain, which while no barrier, did give the room a degree of privacy.

She hesitated and peeped in. It was like stepping out of the twentieth century and back into the time of the Arabian Nights.

The room was lit by ornately-worked lamps of brass

and copper which hung on brackets around the walls.
There were no tables or chairs. The twenty or so people
the room contained sat on rugs and cushions in groups
on the floor.

At the centre of each group was a woven mat on which
lay shallow dishes piled high with mounds of rice, vegetables and spiced meat.

Watching one swarthy man in the group nearest her,
Elyn saw him flick the ends of his keffiyeh, the checked
head-covering, back over his shoulders out of the way.
Then he leaned forward, scooping up a handful of rice
and onions to add to the chunks of meat already on his
plate. To the rice he added another handful of peppers
and tomatoes.

Then he began to eat with his fingers while carrying on
a lively conversation with his friends.

'I thought you were hungry,' Tim murmured in her
ear.

'I am,' Elyn answered.

'Then get along inside, we're holding things up.'

Elyn glanced round and saw behind Tim the Arab who
had welcomed them. Behind him two women in traditional dress, their heads covered, carried brass trays
laden with dishes of steaming food.

Elyn quickly pushed aside the bead curtain and stepped into the room. There was a sudden lull in both eating
and conversation as a score of pairs of eyes studied her.

For one heart-stopping moment Elyn wondered if
there was something wrong with her appearance. Had
she offended local custom in some way? Then she heard
Tim's voice once more.

'See? I told you you looked pretty.'

Unused to compliments, especially in front of a room
full of people, Elyn flushed crimson. Then, just before
the noise resumed its former level, a female voice with a
soft Devon burr called, 'Over here, my dear.'

The familiar sound of English spoken by a friendly
female voice was never so welcome, and Elyn made
her way carefully across the room to where the only

two white faces smiled in greeting.

'Come and sit here, by me.' This cheery invitation came from a plump, motherly woman in her mid-fifties. Her ample curves were clad in black slacks, a yellow shirt and a purple hand-knitted cardigan which had obviously seen better days. She was comfortably seated, like a mother hen, on a nest of cushions. Frizzy grey hair topped a rosy, apple-cheeked face and her wide smile almost caused her periwinkle eyes to disappear completely.

'I'm Maud Barnes and this is my husband Henry,' she announced. 'Hullo there, Tim,' she twinkled over Elyn's shoulder, 'isn't this a lovely surprise.'

'Yes, lovely.' Tim returned the greeting with markedly less enthusiasm than Maud was showing.

'We haven't seen Tim for ages. Here's a couple of cushions, dear.' Maud pushed them towards Elyn. 'You haven't got much padding on your bones, not like me,' she laughed.

Elyn sat down on the cushions and drew her legs up under her. She noticed that both Maud and Henry, despite their ages, sat cross-legged and were obviously quite at ease.

'Are you something to do with the Desert Reclamation Scheme then, dear?' Maud asked Elyn, curiosity burning brightly in her eyes.

'Maud, Henry, this is Elyn Scott,' Tim completed the introductions, 'no, she's not part of our team, though I wish she was.' Tim gave Elyn a long look, which had her colour rising again. 'Actually, she's come to join Alex Davidson at Khalifa Clinic.'

'Is that so?' Maud sounded a little surprised. 'Are you a nurse, dear?'

Elyn shook her head, catching Tim's broad grin from the corner of her eye. 'No, actually I'm a doctor.'

'Well, bless me.' Maud's mouth dropped open in astonishment. 'You don't look old enough, and you're much too pretty.'

'Maud, really,' her husband chided gently. He turned

to Elyn, extending his hand. 'It's a great pleasure to meet you, Dr Scott. I'm sure you'll be a welcome sight to Dr Davidson. He's had far too heavy a work load since the last doctor left.'

Elyn was charmed by Henry Barnes's old-world courtesy. She shook his hand, which like the rest of him was bony. His receding hair was white and combed straight back except where a couple of strands flopped sideways. His eyes, set deep, were full of kindness, and were surrounded by hundreds of tiny wrinkles as though they were permanently screwed up, either in concentration, or against the sun's glare. Elyn guessed him to be about five years older than his wife.

Maud patted her arm. 'You mustn't mind me, dear. I know my tongue runs away with me sometimes, but at my age I like to say what I think.' She chuckled, hunching her plump shoulders, 'Mostly I get away with it.'

Elyn warmed to them both. 'I wish *I* could be as sure of Dr Davidson's welcome as you seem to be,' Elyn said ruefully, 'only it appears there's been a mix-up and he's expecting a male doctor.'

Maud's mouth made a round O. Henry leaned forward, 'Come now, a combination of beauty and brains can only be welcomed,' he said with gentle gallantry.

But Mike hadn't thought so, Elyn remembered, and she hadn't revealed much intelligence at the airport according to her rescuer.

'Well, my dear,' Maud chuckled, 'no matter what Alex says, the patients will be glad to see you. A woman's got a special gift where there's illness. It's something in our nature.'

'You all seem to know each other very well,' Elyn remarked, a little surprised.

'There aren't many Europeans in this area,' Henry explained, 'so we do tend to keep in touch and visit periodically when we can.'

'Maud and Henry are archaeologists,' Tim put in, 'we see them at Kharga quite often.'

'Then I shall look forward to seeing you at the clinic,'

Elyn replied. 'As visitors, not patients,' she added hastily.

'Here's Abdullah,' Maud hitched herself more comfortably on her cushions as the landlord began unloading a large tray of bowls and dishes onto the mat around which they were sitting.

'Have you ordered anything special?' Maud asked Tim, who shook his head. 'Then do share ours. There's far too much for just the two of us and I can't abide waste.' She turned to Elyn. 'Have you ever had Egyptian food before, dear?'

Elyn shook her head. 'I only arrived here a few hours ago.'

'Then you'll love it,' Maud enthused. 'This is couscous. It's a kind of semolina mixed with water and a little oil and steamed. While it's cooking, chopped carrot, turnip, baby marrows, aubergines, onions, tomatoes and chick peas are cooked in the water underneath with meat.'

'It sounds delicious,' Elyn agreed, her mouth watering as Abdullah continued to unload the tray. 'What kind of meat?'

Maud shrugged. 'Oh, it could be mutton, or chicken, or even camel.'

'Oh,' Elyn's smile faltered momentarily, 'that's—er—interesting.' From the corner of her eye she could see Tim watching her, and she was determined not to give him cause for any disparaging remarks about her not being able to adapt to the way of life out here.

'That's not what I said when we first came out here,' Maud laughed, 'was it, Henry?'

Her husband smiled fondly. 'It certainly wasn't. Maud's comments on Egyptian cuisine could have caused an international incident, had she not quickly discovered that she liked it, all of it.'

'I do too,' Maud nodded vigorously. 'Well, you can see,' she patted her hips and sighed. 'Do you know, dear,' she said to Elyn, 'Henry was offered two camels for me by one Bedouin we met.'

Elyn bit her lips, trying to keep a straight face, anxious not to hurt Maud's feelings, but Maud herself capped the story. 'I told Henry to tell him I was worth at least four, but the Bedouin said that was too much because I wasn't fat enough and went on his way.' Maud dissolved in a gale of laughter and Elyn couldn't help but join in. Only Tim seemed slightly reserved.

'What are these other dishes?' Elyn asked.

'That's *chakchouka*, peppers and tomatoes in a sauce made of garlic, onions, red peppers and olive oil.' Maud pointed to each dish in turn. 'That's *dolma*, meat minced with herbs and spices and wrapped in vine leaves, you eat those as well. And that,' she kissed the tops of her chubby fingers, 'is *lham lahon*, mutton and prunes, flavoured with cinnamon and orange flowers. I love it. Then there are the sweets—' She closed her eyes in ecstasy. 'There's one made with the lightest flaky pastry, stuffed with almonds, chopped dates and honey. It simply melts in the mouth,' she pulled a wry face, 'but settles permanently around the waist.' She scooped cous-cous onto her plate, then pushed the dish towards Elyn.

Elyn hesitated. The idea of plunging her hands into the hot food was totally alien to all she had been brought up to believe was good manners.

Henry noticed her reluctance and leaned towards her. 'Use your right hand, Elyn. It's Moslem custom to eat with the right hand, the left is the "unclean" hand, used for washing oneself and so on. Eating with the fingers may seem strange at first, but you'll find the food tastes so good that way, you'll soon be wondering why knives and forks were invented.'

Elyn flashed him a grateful smile and began helping herself. How kind they were, trying to make things easier for her. Fierce hunger, stimulated by the long journey and the appetising smells rising from the hot food, overcame all her reserve, and Elyn joined the others who were already tucking in with dedicated concentration.

'Maud,' she cried in delighted surprise a few moments later, 'you're absolutely right, it's delicious.'

Maud beamed, her cheeks bulging and a tiny dribble of oil running down her chin.

They had finished eating and sat replete and comfortable with tiny cups of mint tea in front of them.

Elyn sighed and tried to stifle a yawn. 'Well, I think I can face the rest of the journey now.'

Henry looked up, surprised, then glanced at Tim. 'Surely you're not thinking of going on tonight, are you?'

Tim shook his head. 'No. We're setting off at first light in the morning. I booked overnight accommodation on the way down.'

Elyn waited for Tim to explain about the predicament they were in over the one bedroom, but he deliberately avoided her gaze. Elyn quickly realised he wasn't going to mention it. He was obviously quite happy about sharing with her. Well, she wasn't, and she didn't like being forced into situations not of her own making.

'But it's presented us with a problem,' Elyn said to Maud, covering her embarrassment with a shy laugh. 'You see, as Dr Davidson had told Tim to expect a man, Tim quite naturally booked only one room and there isn't another to spare.'

'Now, why didn't you say something?' Maud demanded of Tim, who looked slightly uncomfortable.

'I didn't want to bother you with such a trivial matter, Maud. It's just too ridiculous to worry about.'

Maud and Henry exchanged a brief, knowing glance.

'You're right, of course, Tim,' Henry put in quietly, 'no need for a storm in a tea-cup. There's a simple solution for the whole thing.'

'Of course there is,' Maud added patting Elyn's arm, 'you and Henry can change places, my dear.'

'You're sure you wouldn't mind?' Elyn turned from Maud to Henry, who shook his head.

'It's no trouble at all,' he assured her.

'That's settled then,' Maud said comfortably and Elyn

caught Tim's eye. He raised his glass of mint tea in salute with a barely perceptible shrug and a lopsided grin.

'We're off early ourselves,' Maud went on.

'Where are you going?' Elyn turned her attention to Maud, aware that Tim was laughing at her. How old-fashioned he must think her. Well, let him laugh, at least she had avoided a most uncomfortable situation.

'We're going to Abydos,' Maud couldn't disguise her excitement, 'it's one of the most ancient cities in Egypt. It was the centre of the Osiris Cult and the temple there is incredible. Actually, it's seven chapels built side by side, dedicated to seven divine kings who were proclaimed gods. Beneath one of the chapels is a special underground room which was built for celebration of the mysteries of Osiris. It's unique among all the surviving buildings of ancient Egypt.' Maud's eyes were alight with anticipation.

'The friezes on the temple walls are over four thousand years old,' Henry added. 'They are some of the finest Egyptian relief sculptures ever discovered.'

'That amount of time is hard to imagine,' Elyn mused, 'Egypt has always been called the cradle of civilisation, but it's mind-boggling to read how much they actually did know.'

'The first settlers began cultivating Egyptian soil one hundred thousand years ago,' Maud said. 'Before half the world was even inhabited, the Egyptians had chemists and mathematicians. The words chemistry and algebra are of Arabic origin.'

'They were astronomers, invented the astrolabe and developed the science of navigation. They had even developed town planning,' Henry's voice was full of admiration. 'Akhenaten's famous town at Armarma had temples, government offices, police quarters, scribal school and fine housing all laid out in a grid system. That was 3,500 years ago, when England consisted of mud-hut settlements and the Vikings hadn't even thought of invading us yet.'

'I read about a hospital built in Cairo in 872 which had

separate wards for ophthalmia, gynaecology, surgery, dysentery and jaundice,' Elyn said. 'Isn't there also a papyrus which lists forty-eight different wounds and fractures and prescribes treatments for all of them?'

'Someone has been doing their homework,' Tim murmured with an amused grin.

'I know the one you mean,' Maud said, as Elyn flushed. 'It's a copy of one that is supposed to have been first written in 2800 BC.'

Despite a heroic effort Elyn was overcome by a huge yawn.

'Come on, my dear, to bed with you,' Maud clucked. 'You collect your things and let's get some sleep. You've got quite a day ahead of you tomorrow. It's a long drive to Khalifa and then there's your first meeting with your new boss.'

Not quite her first meeting, Elyn thought, but said nothing. As she laid her weary head on the pillow and closed her eyes, she saw once again the stern, chiselled features and enigmatic gaze of Dr Alex Davidson. For there was no doubt in her mind that it was he who had come to her rescue at the airport.

When they met the next day he could hardly help but recognise her. How would he react? How would she cope? Who was the elegant Samina? Where did she fit in?

With the questions whirling in her brain, Elyn fell into an exhausted sleep.

It seemed to Elyn that no sooner had her head touched the pillow, than Maud was shaking her awake.

After a hurried breakfast of bitter coffee and flat pitta bread spread with honey, Elyn was bidding farewell to the Barnes's and clambering into the Land Rover to begin the final stage of her journey.

Tim asked her if she had slept well and she replied that she had. Then, by some tacit unspoken agreement, both avoided the subject of the previous evening and its last-minute change of arrangements.

Elyn was comfortably dressed in cotton shirt and jeans and warm sweater. She gazed sleepily out into the clear turquoise dawn. The air was still cool and fresh, but the temperature was rising every moment as the glowing ball of the sun climbed higher.

The Land Rover devoured the straight strip of dusty road. Beyond it on her left, Elyn could see the railway line which linked upper Egypt with the Nile Delta, and beyond that, the fertile strip of land which edged the river Nile.

Green shoots were already peeping through the freshly deposited layer of rich black mud left each year by the flooding river. The river was still high, it would be several weeks before it receded to its normal level.

Already the peasants, men and women, were working on the land, planting, hoeing, working the shaduf, a weighted device with a bucket at one end which lifted water from the river into irrigation channels.

On Elyn's right, the edge of the road merged into rough, sandy ground which stretched, rock-strewn and barren for several hundred yards, to meet steep sandstone cliffs two hundred feet high which were fluted with drainage channels.

'It's funny,' Elyn said, breaking the silence between them, 'but until I began reading about Egypt I thought that deserts were just sand.'

Tim nodded and grinned. He seemed anxious to be friendly. It was as though he was trying to erase the previous day's happenings and start over again. Elyn was happy to do the same. There was going to be more than enough tension in her meeting with Alex Davidson. She certainly didn't want an awkward journey before she got there. 'Most people do,' Tim said. 'Actually, it's quite amazing just how much deserts do vary. There's gravel surface, which can mean anything from coarse sand to boulders, but is usually flattish pebbles. That's good for driving on. There's sand, which has an infinite variety of colour, density and surface. The best sand for driving on is as fine as baby powder. It often forms a crust. If you keep going fast enough you stay on top, but if you slow down or stop you go through, sometimes axle deep, and it's quite a job to get out. There's salt desert, which is very treacherous and plays havoc with your eyes.'

'How's that?' Elyn asked.

'The glare of the sun on the salt crystals is literally blinding,' Tim replied. 'Another danger that people are often unprepared for is quicksand. That's usually found in dried-out river beds, washes or run-off areas after flash-floods.'

'Floods?' Elyn was surprised. 'How do those occur? I thought the whole point about a desert was its dryness.'

'That's true. Rainfall over desert is almost non-existent,' Tim agreed. 'There may not be a single drop for several years. Then atmospheric conditions up to a hundred miles away will cause sudden heavy rainstorms which can make a dry river-bed a raging torrent several feet high in minutes.'

Despite the growing warmth Elyn shivered. 'That's frightening.'

Tim nodded grimly. 'It certainly is. It happened at Kharga seven years ago and the devastation was terrible. Several children were drowned, livestock was lost and three old people were killed when their houses collapsed.'

'How does it happen?' Elyn was horrified.

'The ground is baked too hard to absorb that sudden deluge of water from the sky,' Tim explained, 'so it pours from the hills into the gullies and wadis, the river-beds, to find the lowest point.'

Elyn shuddered again. 'How is it that so much of Egypt is desert? My book said that there were once oak and cedar forests growing on the Saharan Highlands and that huge areas were planted with enough corn and wheat to feed the Roman Empire. What happened?'

Tim shrugged. 'Partly climatic changes and more recently, man. We're talking about the past 65 million years, don't forget. During that time the borders of the

Sahara have expanded and retreated many times. Sahara is actually the plural of the Arabic word for desert, *sahra*. It contains half the desert surface of the world and consists of all the different types of desert I mentioned earlier. The prevailing winds are driving the dune fields of the western desert towards the Nile Valley. The dunes cover roads and bury telephone poles. In one place the railway has been re-routed around one huge dune, but the sand has continued to advance and now the bypass is also threatened.'

'It's incredible that such tiny grains can cause so much destruction,' Elyn murmured.

'There are a lot of them,' Tim remarked drily. 'As usual, man is greatly responsible for the encroachment of the desert.'

'How?'

'By chopping down trees for fuel, by cultivating to death the lands that fringe the desert, by allowing sheep and camels to graze every bit of bush and scrub.'

'But surely there are some good years?' Elyn pointed out, 'when the rain does come, for instance.'

Tim nodded, but his face remained grim. 'Yes, and when it does and plants will grow, the land is over-cultivated and sucked dry of all nourishment, so that the next drought is even more devastating. You see, drought feeds on itself. As vegetation is stripped from the land, the surface dries out and reflects more of the sun's heat. That alters the temperature of the atmosphere and suppresses rainfall.'

'But that can't be the only cause, surely?' Elyn asked.

Tim shrugged. 'There are some scientists who believe that increased dust and other pollutants in the atmosphere are causing, or certainly aggravating, changes in the climate which favour desert conditions.'

Elyn thought for a moment. 'There was something on TV about aerosol sprays releasing particles into the atmosphere which are destroying the ozone layer.'

Tim nodded. 'That's right. The propellants in the aerosols are causing a layer of carbon dioxide to build up on the earth's atmosphere. So the heat from the earth's surface can't escape out into space.'

'Is that what they call the "Greenhouse effect"?' Elyn asked.

Tim nodded and they talked on. He explained his team's long-term plans for reclaiming the desert. Elyn was completely absorbed and listened carefully, putting questions now and again.

They stopped briefly for a quick lunch of goat's cheese, pitta bread and dates, washed down with fruit juice from Tim's vacuum jug.

Elyn was glad to get out of the jolting Land Rover and stretch her legs for a few minutes. Her sweater had long since been abandoned, but the heat, like a burning, heavy weight on her skull, soon drove her back into the vehicle, and they were once more on their way.

'Tim, you talked about driving on the different desert surfaces,' Elyn said, 'but I thought camels were the main form of transport.'

'Romantic notions of the East again,' Tim teased, 'Lawrence of Arabia and *The Desert Song* have a lot to answer for. They did use to be. There were well-worn routes across the Sahara used by caravans numbering a hundred or more, carrying spices, cotton, coffee and precious stones. But as sea and air travel developed and was obviously more practical, the caravans became a thing of the past.'

Elyn sighed. 'I suppose that makes sense, in practical terms, but it does seem a shame. There must have been a sense of timelessness about travelling with a caravan.'

Tim grunted. 'It was slow, uncomfortable, dirty and dangerous. There were also bands of brigands on the lookout for easy pickings. Anyway, have you ever been close to a camel?'

Elyn shook her head.

'Just be thankful,' Tim warned, 'they're bad-tempered, smelly, unsociable creatures.'

'Maybe,' Elyn allowed, 'but they have beautiful eyes and fantastically long lashes.'

Tim gazed heavenwards. 'Women,' he muttered despairingly.

It was about three in the afternoon when Tim turned the Land Rover off the main road and they began climbing into the hills.

Elyn was sticky with perspiration and fine dust. She felt grubby and dishevelled and as each mile carried her closer to the clinic and Alex Davidson, her apprehension grew.

There was nothing to which she could turn her thoughts. Tim had lapsed into silence to concentrate on driving and once they reached the plateau, the view was as barren and desolate as a lunar landscape. Still the sun beat down. The inside of the metal-bodied Land Rover was like an oven. The air going into Elyn's lungs burned. Her mouth was dry and her tongue felt like leather. She could see huge drops of perspiration running down Tim's neck and soaking into his shirt. Behind the sunglasses his eyes were screwed up against the glare.

Numb with heat and fatigue, Elyn sank into a sort of doze. She was quite startled when Tim announced. 'We're almost there.'

Elyn looked about her. She could see nothing but rocks and dust and low sandstone hillocks. She wondered how Tim could tell the difference between these rocks and those they had been passing for the last two hours.

Elyn reached into her bag and took out her comb and a plastic container of cologne-soaked pads, silently blessing Aunt Connie for her thoughtfulness. She took them even on the shortest trips and had slipped the box into Elyn's bag as she was leaving.

Wiping off the grime Elyn was immediately refreshed by the cooling effect of the spirit on her skin. As she raked the comb through her damp curls, she caught Tim grinning sideways at her.

'Hoping to impress the boss?' he teased.

Elyn forced a smile in return, hoping her sudden throat-drying nervousness was well hidden. 'This is for *my* benefit, not Dr Davidson's,' she retorted. 'If you were in my place, wouldn't you try to smarten up a little?'

'I suppose so,' he admitted.

'Besides,' Elyn went on, 'from what you've told me about Dr Davidson, the fact that I'm a woman is already against me, so even if I greeted him in a bikini with a rose between my teeth, I doubt if he'd notice, much less be impressed.'

'Well, I certainly would,' Tim whistled. 'I'd jump under the first passing camel so that I could experience your tender ministrations.'

'Then you'd be wasting your time,' Elyn said lightly, her heart beginning to thud unevenly as the dreaded meeting drew closer, 'Hit-and-run camel injuries are strictly outpatients. There's probably a big buxom nurse with hands of iron and a heart of gold just waiting for you.'

'I always said doctors were unfeeling, cold-hearted creatures,' Tim mourned. 'It could all have been so different. He flashed a meaningful glance at her. 'If you hadn't met Maud and Henry—'

But Elyn wasn't listening. They had just rounded a bend between two low hills and, suddenly, there below them was a broad shallow valley that ran as far as she could see.

Tall date palms stood in elegant groups. Stands of acacia and cassia trees laden with flowers offered welcome shade. The very sight of the lush greenery after so much barren rock was balm to Elyn's eyes. The small mud-brick houses of the oasis-dwellers nestled among the trees and bushes. The rectangular design with small courtyard and stairs leading to a flat roof had remained unchanged for two thousand years.

Sheep and goats, watched over by young boys, nibbled at rough scrub and patches of clover on the edges of the oasis. Geese and chickens wandered freely, pecking at the sandy soil. Several long-legged, dust-coloured camels were tethered beside a stone trough. They sat with their legs folded beneath them, exposing as little body surface as possible to the sun. Flat heads atop long necks gazed arrogantly around as they chewed the cud.

Hungrily Elyn absorbed it all, then she looked up the valley. Surrounded by palms, and glistening white in the afternoon sun, stood a large, single-storey H-shaped building, Khalifa Clinic. Then Elyn noticed something which made her gasp.

Inside the clinic compound, which was surrounded by a strong fence to keep out the wandering animals, were beds of flowers, jasmine, violets and narcissus.

'Oh, how lovely,' Elyn was entranced. 'I never expected to see flowers. I thought all the water would be used for food crops.'

'It was Alex Davidson's idea,' Tim informed her, putting the Land Rover in gear and starting down the track to the oasis. 'He says the flowers are of great therapeutic value to the patients. He's always asking us to recommend plants he could try growing here. Also, he says they have religious significance.'

'In what way?' Elyn was surprised. It was difficult to imagine the terse, busy man she had encountered having time or interest in such trivial details as flowers.

'It's one of the traditions of Islam that bliss on earth and in heaven is to be found in a fragrant garden. Many of the Bedouin have never even seen a garden and Alex is convinced that the flowers do more to overcome their suspicion of the clinic than all the verbal persuasion he might try.'

Elyn nodded. What a strange man this Dr Alex Davidson was. What a brain he must have to be able to encompass not only the medical and surgical requirements of the clinic, but the administration as well, and still have time to study the beliefs and ways of life of both the oasis-dwellers and the nomadic tribes who passed this way.

'He's got two old men working full time on the shrubs and flowers and they are training two more. They con-

sider it a great honour and their passport to Paradise,'
Tim shouted above the roaring engine.

'What a lovely thought,' Elyn called back as they drew
up outside the compound.

Tim jumped out of the Land Rover, leaving the engine
running, and came round to Elyn's side to open her
door.

She clambered out stiffly, her shirt sticking to her
back, and stood uncertainly.

'Aren't you coming in?' she asked, striving to keep the
hope from her voice. The meeting might be a little easier
if there was someone else present.

Tim pulled Elyn's case from the back of the Land
Rover and set it by her feet. 'No,' he shook his head, 'I
said I'd deliver the new doctor and that I've done. Alex
is probably too busy to stop and chat, not that he's got
much small talk anyway.'

Elyn sensed something in Tim's tone. 'Don't you get
on together?' she ventured, anxious to discover anything
she could which might help her understand the dark,
taciturn man with whom she was was to work for the next
six months, assuming he allowed her to stay.

'We get along,' Tim said briefly, obviously unwilling
to say more. 'I've got to get back to Kharga this afternoon. We've already lost a week on the new planning
programme.' He grinned at her. 'But I'll be back. I guess
we got off on the wrong foot. I tried to rush my fences
and all that.' He scuffed his feet in the dust and then
glanced up at her sheepishly. 'No offence intended.' He
stuck out his hand.

Elyn grasped it. 'None taken,' she smiled.

Tim tilted his head and stared hard at her, a quizzical
frown on his face. 'Will you bloom here, I wonder? A
beautiful desert flower? Or will the heat and the dust
shrivel you up and make you scuttle back to England?'
He grinned again. 'Only time will tell.' Leaning forward
he gave Elyn a quick peck on the cheek. 'Good luck, Dr
Scott, I'll be seeing you soon.'

'Thanks, Tim,' Elyn smiled, but the thudding of her

heart was caused more by the immediate prospect of facing Alex Davidson, than by Tim's affectionate gesture.

Tim turned away and went round the front of the Land Rover. He opened the door and was about to climb in. 'You should be glad I'm not staying,' he called. 'I would be trying very hard to keep your mind off your work. Anyway, there's no way Alex can send you back for at least a week.'

With a final wave he slammed the door and roared off down the valley in a cloud of dust.

Elyn stared after him for a few moments, then, taking a deep breath, she picked up her case. Hitching her bag over her shoulder she opened the gate and entered the compound.

Crossing the flattened sandy soil, Elyn walked up the steps to a deep shady verandah and in through the main doors. She was in a wide passage. The walls were painted a soft green and the floor was tiled. In front of her were three white-painted doors.

As she was wondering what to do, the door on her left opened and a nurse emerged, dressed in a scrub suit of white tunic and trousers, her hair completely covered by her white theatre cap. She was short and had the fleshy build of most middle-aged Egyptian women. As she caught sight of Elyn her eyebrows lifted in surprise and then she nodded politely.

'*Salamu aleikum*,' she gave the traditional greeting, 'peace to you.'

'Er—*aleikum as-salaam*,' Elyn replied hastily, then reverted to English. 'Could you tell me where I will find Dr Davidson, please?'

The nurse looked puzzled. 'Dr Davidson in theatre,' she replied. Her English was heavily accented but quite fluent, and Elyn was grateful. She knew her Arabic was adequate for only the briefest conversation.

'You come wrong time,' the nurse explained. 'Outpatients in morning, every day in morning,' she repeated and tried very gently to edge Elyn towards the doors.

Elyn stood her ground. 'I am Dr Scott,' she introduced herself. 'I am Dr Davidson's new assistant.'

The nurse's face remained impassive, but Elyn saw the sudden hostility in her eyes.

'Please, you wait, I fetch Dr Davidson,' the nurse turned to go back through the door. Just then it opened.

'Jehan, I've put him on a dextran and glucose drip to counteract shock.' The unforgettable deep voice sent a quiver down Elyn's spine and she stiffened.

'Tell Mohammed the patient is ready for the ward now, and make sure he doesn't dislodge the tube. I'll write up the morphine dosage when—'

Alex Davidson strode out into the passage and stopped short. His brows drew together in a swift frown and his green eyes were glacial as he fixed Elyn with a stare that made her flinch inwardly.

'What in God's name are you doing here?' he demanded.

Elyn bit her lip. She had not expected a warm welcome, but this was far worse than she had imagined. He looked thunderous.

Summoning all her courage, Elyn straightened her back. Tilting her chin defiantly as she looked up at him, she held out her hand.

'This is quite a surprise for me too, Dr Davidson. I am Dr Elyn Scott, your new assistant.'

Alex Davidson stared at her in open disbelief. He pulled the white cap from his dark, rumpled hair, shrugged out of his stained operating gown and handed them both to the nurse.

'Jehan, see to him,' he nodded in the direction of the door through which he'd just come, 'then ask Mohammed to set up a saline IV for Hamid in bed three. His sodium output is still too high. As he can't take fluids by mouth yet we must replace the salts he's losing.'

Alex Davidson gave his instructions clearly and quickly and the nurse nodded and hurried away.

He returned his gaze to Elyn and his face grew even grimmer. Ignoring her extended hand, he ran his fingers through the sweat-dampened hair, flexing his broad shoulders as if to ease their stiffness.

'You? My new assistant? What sort of joke is this?'

CHAPTER THREE

ELYN's cheeks flamed. 'If you mean what happened at the airport, that could have happened to anyone.'

'As I recall, you kept insisting that you were quite capable of taking care of yourself,' Alex Davidson glowered, 'though the opposite seemed to be the case.' He waved a dismissive hand. 'However, that is not what I meant—'

Elyn let her hand fall to her side. 'Excuse me, Dr Davidson,' she interrupted with thumping heart and knees like jelly. She had to make him understand. Despite that first impression, she was not a silly, helpless female. Her intuition warned her that no matter how frightening the prospect she must stand up to this man, risk his fury. If she backed off or gave way, she was lost.

'Tim Preston told me there had been a mix-up. I'm very sorry about it, but I really don't see that it need be a problem.'

Elyn tried a confident smile, aware that she was blushing under his scrutiny and furious with herself for not being able to prevent it. Why did he have this ability to unnerve her?

Alex Davidson observed her in silence for a few moments, his forbidding expression making Elyn feel like a naughty pupil called before the Head.

'Oh,' he said, caustically, 'so you don't think it need be a problem.' His face darkened. 'Young woman, you don't know what you're talking about. Come to my office.' He turned on his heel and started down the corridor, leaving Elyn to follow.

Snatching up her suitcase she hurried after him. Charm certainly wasn't his great weakness, Elyn fumed inwardly.

His large desk was cluttered with books, folders and

piles of papers. Alex Davidson walked round behind it. Indicating a chair between the desk and the wall for Elyn, he sat down.

Pushing aside some files, he leaned his elbows on the desk.

'There's no question of you remaining here as my assistant,' he stated brusquely. 'In fact, there's no chance of you remaining here at all. I shall make arrangements to have you flown back to Cairo as soon as possible.'

'But I don't understand,' Elyn cried, 'why can't I stay?'

'You know perfectly well why.' He made no effort to conceal his exasperation and leaned back in his chair.

'No I don't,' Elyn retorted. 'Unless you deal exclusively with male patients, which eliminates mothers, babies and all women in between, there is a need for a woman doctor, if my sex is the problem.'

'It's not that simple,' he scowled, 'conditions out here are rough, it's no picnic, and my assistant needs to be able to switch from medicine to surgery, from children's diseases to psychiatry, all in the course of a day. Besides,' he snapped, 'the last woman I had inflicted upon me was totally unsuitable.'

'I'm sorry you've had staff problems,' Elyn replied, her voice quite calm, revealing none of the turmoil inside her, 'but you can't condemn all women doctors just because of one.'

With a smooth, panther-like movement, Alex leaned forward, his powerful shoulders and icy gaze menacing even though he remained seated.

'Listen carefully,' he grated, 'I am in charge here. My word is law. I can do *exactly* as I please, and don't forget that.'

Shock tingled down Elyn's spine. He really meant it.

'Forgive me,' she murmured, 'I was not questioning your authority, only your sense of fairness.' His eyes flickered and one dark brow lifted as she hurried on.

'I applied for this job because I want it very much. I

already knew quite a lot about the conditions, and Tim Preston went to great lengths to tell me more. I still want this job.' Elyn took a deep breath and screwed up her courage. 'Look, it would take you at least a month to replace me. You would have to refer back to the short list, there'd be correspondence, interviews and so on. My qualifications were obviously acceptable when you thought I was a man. Give me one month as a trial period. If, at the end of it, you have any reason to doubt my professional ability, then replace me.'

Elyn ran out of breath, and crimson-cheeked at her own boldness, she tried to give an impression of calm confidence as she waited anxiously for his reaction.

Alex leaned back. Tapping his fingers on the desk top, and swivelling his chair fractionally from side to side, he studied her.

'Are you religious?' The question was abrupt and totally unexpected.

'I do have beliefs,' Elyn said uncertainly.

'But you aren't attached to a particular denomination?' he pressed.

Elyn shook her head. 'No, I've been to different churches at different times in my life, but I never felt strongly enough to commit myself to any one of them.'

'Too busy a social life?' he asked pointedly.

'Too much studying,' Elyn returned. She was confused. 'Surely my lack of religious commitment doesn't count against me?'

His grim mask softened momentarily and the lines on either side of his wide mouth deepened.

'As a matter of fact, it's a point in your favour. My last assistant was a devout member of some obscure but intense denomination. That in itself was quite harmless and her own business. But she decided to "spread the word" among the patients and staff here with a zeal that would have made a missionary cringe. That was unforgivable.' His anger was terrifying.

'We are guests in this country and apart from being an appalling breach of good manners, her activities almost

destroyed the months of groundwork we had put in to
build up trust between ourselves and the local peoples
who are all Moslem.' He glanced at Elyn. 'I trust you
have no such calling?'

'None at all,' Elyn replied honestly.

'Unfortunately you are right about the time it would
take to replace you,' he said thoughtfully, 'so I want to
make something crystal clear. We occupy a unique
position here, and if I decide to give you a trial, which is
by no means certain, you will respect the practices of
Islam, which is a whole way of life, not simply a relig-
ion, and keep your private opinions and beliefs to yourself.'

'But of course,' Elyn said stiffly. What on earth did he
think she was going to do? Her medical duties, especially
under his critical gaze, would keep her fully occupied.
Besides, she was a firm believer in a person's religious
leanings being their own business.

'Tell me, what made you decide to come out here, to
the back of beyond?' Alex's expression was quizzical. 'If
you wanted to change, why didn't you go into research?
Or, if it was the lure of foreign parts, why not one of the
wealthy Saudi clinics with all the latest in equipment and
technology?' An eyebrow lifted. 'Are you running away
from something?' His eyes bored into hers. 'Or someone? A broken love affair perhaps?'

Elyn's cheeks flamed. 'My private life is my own
business, Dr Davidson. I am not running away from
anything or anyone. I chose Khalifa because I prefer
people to test-tubes. I feel that medicine has become
too dependant on technology to the detriment of the
patients. Even in diagnostics, machines and computers
are taking over. I'm not saying there isn't a place for
them.'

Elyn was finding it difficult to explain herself under his
sceptical gaze.

'An illness or a disease is not a thing on its own, it
happens to a person. I feel that as doctors we should take
more interest in the whole person, his background,

family, job, all the things that make him or her the person they are. It's not enough to prescribe pills for a set of symptoms.' Elyn moistened her lips and twined her fingers together. 'To be a doctor out here, where there is a chance to make a real difference to people's lives, to help them help themselves, and to relieve unnecessary suffering, that for me is what medicine is all about.'

Alex's mouth twisted sardonically. 'Another social conscience and saviour of mankind. I wonder what tune you'd sing with a clinic full of people and all too few of the facilities you appear to despise.'

'I should probably feel frustrated,' Elyn admitted, 'but I still think that preventive care, with attention to diet, personal hygiene and sanitation would greatly reduce the incidence of disease, though of course it takes time. At least most of the illness out here is not self-inflicted, like the results of drinking and smoking and drug dependence.'

Alex looked at her more closely, as if seeing something he hadn't noticed before.

'Well, you do at least appear to have the right attitude for a job like this,' he allowed grudgingly, 'but attitude and theories are not enough. Performance is what counts, and my standards are high.'

His piercing gaze rivetted Elyn to her chair. 'As I seem to be stuck with you, you might as well be useful. We'll see if your practical ability matches your paper qualifications.' He leaned forward. 'Let's get one thing straight, no allowances will be made for the fact that you are a woman.'

'I expect none,' Elyn countered quickly. She had won. She was staying, at least temporarily. He would find no fault with her work, of that she was determined.

'What are the main diseases endemic here?' she asked, anxious to bring the conversation back to professional matters. 'The information in my medical textbooks applies to the Nile Valley and delta where most of the population is concentrated.

'TB, hookworm, enteritis, bilharzia, trachoma,' Alex ticked them off on his fingers. 'This clinic has been set up as an advance post of the new development scheme of desert reclamation.'

'Tim was telling me about it,' Elyn put in quickly. 'I gather the development is to extend from Kharga up to this oasis and then out into the desert.'

Alex's mouth curved in a contemptuous smile. 'Tim Preston certainly has made a good impression. Just as a matter of interest, were you both comfortable last night?'

For a moment Elyn didn't understand, then anger flared. Alex had told Tim to book a room for overnight, expecting a man. Alex knew nothing of the arrangement with Maud and Henry and from the expression on his face he was insinuating that she and Tim had shared not only a room, but a bed. How dare he? No matter what his opinion of Tim Preston, he had no right to jump to conclusions about her. Elyn was furious.

'Speaking for myself, I was very comfortable, thank you,' Elyn said tightly. 'The food was delicious and I slept marvellously. You were telling me about the clinic?' She tilted her head, meeting his gaze levelly. Let him think what he liked, she owed him no explanation. What a rude, overbearing, supercilious man he was.

Alex's face registered surprise as he held her gaze for a second or two, then his expression hardened, and he nodded slightly as if in confirmation of his own thoughts.

'We aim to treat not only the oasis-dwellers, but also the nomadic Berber and Tuareg tribesmen who still travel the desert with their families and their herds of sheep, goats and camels. Their way of life is rapidly becoming impossible and many of them are settling. Unfortunately they have little immunity to the diseases with which they come into contact. Our purpose is to provide medical aid, health education and maternity and child welfare services.'

Alex pushed back his chair and stood up. 'Come and

look at this,' he indicated a framed plan on the wall behind his desk.

Elyn joined him. He towered above her. The top of her head just reached his chin. She was suddenly very aware of his size and strength, of his rugged maleness.

He looked down into her eyes with a mocking smile, as if reading her thoughts.

Elyn felt warmth rising in her cheeks and looked away quickly, angry with herself and with him. She didn't even like him.

'As you see,' he tapped the plan, 'we have three wards, an X-ray department, a small lab and pharmacy combined, operating theatre and maternity unit and a large outpatients and casualty unit.' He pointed them out in turn.

'We treat as many patients as possible as outpatients, limiting admissions to absolute emergencies. What facilities we have are basic, with none of the refinements you are probably used to. This clinic is still very much on trial as far as the Government and WHO are concerned. For instance, the theatre has no ancillary sterilising or anaesthetic rooms, and there is only one scrub and changing room for the doctors, you see? Already the problems begin,' he said brusquely.

'I can change and scrub with the theatre nurses,' Elyn anticipated him quickly.

'Which is not only against protocol, but will complicate any pre-op discussion regarding anaesthesia and operating technique, especially in an emergency, which most of our operations are,' he snapped. Alex ran impatient fingers through his rumpled hair. 'This simply isn't going to work,' he growled, 'I was a fool to think it could.'

'What happens about food for the patients and staff?' Elyn asked desperately, steering the conversation back to the clinic facilities.

'There's a kitchen behind the clinic building, also a laundry and the residences. Which brings me to our second problem. See how quickly they arise?' He leaned against the wall, half obscuring the plan, and folded his arms. He was so close in the cramped space between the desk and the wall in the small office that Elyn could feel the warmth emanating from him, tinged with antiseptic and soap. She could see crisp dark hair curling at the neck of his scrub suit and the shadow of stubble on his lean jaw. His powerful masculinity was disturbing.

'Had you been the man I expected, you would have shared my house.' He paused, deliberately, and Elyn glanced up at him, her eyes wide.

'However, as things are,' he went on with a gusty sigh, 'I suppose I shall have to put you in one of the guest houses.'

Like an unwanted package, Elyn bristled.

'Thank you,' she murmured quickly. At least he had offered the alternative before she had had to ask. It was going to be difficult enough working with this prickly, demanding perfectionist, knowing every moment she was under observation. There was no way she could have shared quarters with him. She needed somewhere of her own to retreat to. A private haven away from the storms she instinctively knew were inevitable, away from those penetrating eyes which would not miss a single error or hesitation.

But apart from all that there was a magnetism about him, a masculine forcefulness, which, combined with his derisive mockery, completely unsettled Elyn. She had never before encountered a man like him, and she was finding it difficult to cope.

Alex glanced at his watch.

'There's a patient I must check on. I'll get someone to show you to your quarters.' He moved towards her and Elyn stepped back so quickly that she stumbled. Alex's hand shot out and steadied her.

His touch was like an electric shock to Elyn whose nerves were already stretched.

Her reaction was not lost on Alex. 'Don't panic, Dr Scott.' He gave a wolfish grin, 'I'm not about to ravish you, it's too hot and I'm rather too busy.'

Elyn blushed furiously as he passed her, and, unable to think of a suitably crushing reply, she busied herself with her bag and suitcase as Alex opened a door connecting with one of the wards.

He spoke in Arabic to a young trainee nurse who was dressed in white tunic and trousers. Her hair was tied back and covered with a white cotton cloth knotted at the nape of her neck.

The girl listened with lowered eyes to Alex's rapid instructions, then politely motioned Elyn to follow her.

'Be back here in half an hour.' Alex threw the words over his shoulder as he strode past Elyn into the ward.

Biting back an angry retort, Elyn followed the girl down the tiled passage and out through a back door. The heat struck her like a blow and she felt sweat break out all over her body.

Asking Elyn to wait, the girl hurried to one of the buildings facing them. By the steam puffing from the windows and the smell of soap, Elyn deduced it was the laundry. She was back within moments and they continued past a residential block which, the girl explained in heavily-accented English, was divided lengthways with one half for the two sisters and nurses who lived in, and the other for the two paramedics who drove the ambulance.

Then the young nurse pointed out Alex Davidson's bungalow. It looked quite large for a man on his own. But, Elyn reasoned, it might have been built with the idea of the doctor in charge being a married man, perhaps with a family.

Was Alex Davidson married, Elyn wondered. Then, a flash of memory recalled the airport, and the beautiful Egyptian on his arm. Perhaps she was the future Mrs Davidson. If that was so, then the elegant Samina had Elyn's sympathy. He would be a very difficult and demanding man to live with. In fact, Elyn thought to herself, marriage to Alex Davidson would be hell on earth.

Suddenly she realised the direction of her thoughts.

Thrusting them hurriedly from her mind, she concentrated on the small building towards which they were heading.

Unlocking the door, the nurse pushed it wide and gestured for Elyn to precede her.

The guest house was small and compact. The front door led into a tiny white-painted sitting room, sparsely furnished with a small red settee, some book shelves, a dark wooden table and an upright chair. Two small patterned rugs covered the tiled floor. An oil lamp was bracketed to the wall, but there was also an electric light on the ceiling with a plain white shade.

Through this room was a small kitchen with a gas ring run from a cylinder, a tiny fridge, two cupboards, a stone sink and a minute table beneath which was a stool.

Following her guide Elyn came next to the tiny shower room and loo, next to which was the only bedroom.

This was also painted white and contained a single bed with a blue coverlet spread over the mattress, a shelf below a mirror and a dark wood wardrobe. A sandalwood chest at the foot of the bed caught Elyn's eyes. It was a work of art, beautifully carved and strangely opulent in the starkly functional room. The fragrance of the wood permeated the room.

Lifting the lid of the chest, the nurse took out two woollen blankets and a pillow which she placed on the bed.

'Maid bring sheets and towels from laundry,' she explained.

Elyn was about to ask how she was to obtain a maid when there was a knock at the front door and a young Arab girl of about fourteen entered, her arms full of clean linen. She glanced shyly up at Elyn from huge limpid brown eyes.

'This Nefra, she your maid,' the nurse explained. 'Make bed, keep house clean, do washing and all things. What you need you tell her, she do it for you. She good, honest girl from good family. She my cousin. I go now, Sister need me on ward.'

Elyn suppressed a smile. 'Thank you for all your help,' she said gravely.

The nurse bowed politely and, exchanging a few soft words with Nefra, hurried out.

Elyn lifted her case onto the chest and opened it as Nefra began making up the bed. She was quick and deft and as soon as she'd finished she came to Elyn's side and gently pushed her away.

'I do for you, put away. That my job. You take shower, feel better,' she nodded and made fluttering movements with her hands as if to shoo Elyn out.

For Elyn the thought of cool water on her body was deliciously inviting. She was hot and sticky and tired. Taking the fresh towel Nefra handed her, she picked up her toilet-bag and left the little Arab girl to her self-appointed task.

Twenty minutes later, her bubbly curls still damp from the shower, Elyn was retracing her steps from the little bungalow to the clinic building.

She had exchanged her jeans and shirt for a pale green cotton dress, but had retained her sandals. The thought of stockings or tights and proper shoes in that heat was unbearable.

Alex Davidson glanced at his watch as she entered his office, but apart from raising one eyebrow he made no comment.

Elyn was glad she was a couple of minutes early. It had been the quickest shampoo, shower and change of clothes she had ever made. She was determined not to give him the slightest reason to criticise.

Alex gave her a brief glance which raked her from head to toe and left her feeling as though she'd been scanned by a laser.

'That dress is totally unsuitable,' he said curtly. 'I'll see that you're issued with "whites" for tomorrow. They'll be less offensive to patients or staff. What size shoes do you take?'

'Six,' Elyn stuttered, stunned by his scathing remark. How could he say the shirtwaist style with short sleeves

was offensive? Still, she acknowledged, she had much to
learn about local customs and dress.

'We keep a supply of canvas shoes for the nurses and
auxiliaries,' he went on briskly. 'They are easily steril-
ised and are safer and more hygienic than open sandals.'
He fixed her with a cutting stare.

'Didn't you do any preliminary reading before you
jumped on that 'plane?'

'Of course I did,' Elyn retorted hotly.

'Then tell me what you know about hookworm disease,' he demanded.

Elyn was puzzled but thought quickly. 'It's caused by
the larvae of a parasite which reach the lungs via the
bloodstream. Then they pass up to the epiglottis and are
swallowed. When they reach the small intestine they
attach themselves to the mucous lining by means of
hooks and feed by sucking blood and grow into worms
about one inch long.'

Pausing for breath, she looked up expectantly, knowing her recall was perfect. But his expression was disparaging.

'And how do the larvae get into the body in the first
place?'

Elyn bit her lip and frowned. 'The eggs are passed in
the faeces and develop into larvae in the soil,' she
recited, then suddenly it dawned and she closed her eyes
in mortification as the rest of the textbook paragraph
came into her brain in letters of fire. How *could* she have
forgotten?

'Go on,' his voice was icy and relentless, 'tell me the
rest.'

With cheeks flaming, unable to meet his eyes, Elyn
took a deep breath. 'The larvae can penetrate the intact
skin of bare feet,' she spoke clearly, but inside she
cringed with embarrassment and shame. 'This occurs
mostly during contact with contaminated soil.'

She broke off and stared at her open sandals. She
should have remembered. This was a clinic. Patients
with hookworm would be treated here. Though unlike-

ly, it was just possible that eggs or larvae from the earth-dusted bare feet of patients could be brushed off onto the floors. How could she have been so thoughtless and forgetful. She had talked so glibly about preventative care.

Surely Alex Davidson would not miss this opportunity to crow. Elyn's shoulders slumped as she waited for him to pour out his contempt, and to point out how unsuitable she was yet again.

'I suppose you're tired and hungry.'

To Elyn's amazement his voice held none of the disparagement of a few moments ago. It was an odd blend of exasperation and something else, something that Elyn could not recognise.

'It has been rather a long day,' she admitted.

'I was going to show you over the clinic and introduce you to the staff this evening, but,' he glanced at his watch, 'I suppose it can wait until the morning.' His tone reverted to its familiar brusqueness. 'I doubt you'd take much in. Go and have a meal. Your maid will have left essentials in the fridge, or you can get hot food from the kitchen. Then get an early night. If I'm to be stuck with you, even for a short time,' he added pointedly, 'you'll have to earn your keep. So be in my office at seven-thirty in the morning.'

He turned and strode away with the lithe grace of a jungle cat.

Elyn followed him down the passage, her fists clenched in frustration. He was infuriating, impossible, utterly unpredictable. One minute as hard and cold as steel, the next revealing a flash of humour or compassion totally at odds with his normal taciturnity.

As much as she wanted the job and was determined to keep it, Elyn couldn't help wondering what it was going to cost her in terms of frustration and rage at his attitude towards her. What had she done to deserve such behaviour, which seemed to waver between supercilious contempt and amused irritation?

As she returned his brief parting nod, Elyn gritted her

teeth. She would show Dr Alex Davidson. She was twenty-five years old, an independent woman and a fully qualified doctor. She had worked hard to get her medical degree and she would work even harder to prove herself right for this job.

She was not an incompetent idiot, but nor was she prepared to massage his ego, by playing the adoring slave, grateful to sit at the feet of the master and glean what crumbs of wisdom and knowledge he deigned to toss her way.

Closing her front door with unaccustomed violence, Elyn saw Nefra's dark head peep round from the kitchen. As she recognised Elyn, Nefra stepped quickly into the room and putting her palms together bowed formally.

'*As-salaamu aleikum, ya sitti doktor*,' she greeted in her soft voice.

Elyn returned the greeting, immediately charmed out of her temper by the girl's sweetness and warm welcome.

'You need not address me as Lady Doctor, Nefra,' she explained gently, 'my name is Elyn.'

The girl was horrified.

'Cannot address you so,' she waved horrified hands. 'Dr Davidson he be much angry. But I can say "*hanem*". It say madam. That good, yes?'

'That's fine,' Elyn smiled, conceding defeat.

'You sit now,' Nefra pointed to the settee, 'I bring food, ready now.'

Elyn sank gratefully onto the settee and moments later Nefra brought in a tray containing a plate of cous-cous with peppers, onions and tomatoes, a dish of fresh dates, apricots, grapes and figs, and a small piece of goat's cheese.

'Coffee on low gas, *hanem*. No wash dishes, I do in morning. Yes.'

'Thank you, Nefra,' Elyn looked at the food and her mouth watered in anticipation. 'This looks delicious.'

The girl glowed with pleasure. 'I go now. Back early in morning. Get breakfast for you.'

'There's no need,' Elyn began. 'I can—'

'Please, *hanem*, this my job. If I no do, Dr Davidson say you no like me, not happy with work—' the girl's full lips trembled and tears welled in her limpid eyes.

'We mustn't upset Dr Davidson, must we?' Elyn murmured through clenched teeth. 'That's fine, Nefra, you come in the morning. I promise I won't do a thing.'

The girl gave a radiant smile and, bowing gracefully, slipped out.

Elyn sighed, then sitting down at the table she began her meal. As the hot food comforted and restored her, she began to relax. By the time she had finished eating all Elyn wanted to do was slide between cool sheets and sleep.

Night had descended with a suddenness that Elyn had been too tired to notice. She drew the curtains and switched on the lights. She would have preferred lamplight, but as she was going straight to bed, it seemed wasteful to light them.

Elyn was in her nightie and had just washed her face. She was brushing her hair when a sudden knock at the door made her jump. Snatching up a thin cotton robe, she pulled it on and padded barefoot to the door.

'Who is it?' she demanded warily.

'Alex, Alex Davidson,' came the impatient reply.

Elyn opened the door. 'Yes?'

There had been no twilight as in English evenings. One moment the sun had been there, a blood-red ball low in the sky, the next it had vanished below the hills and darkness had fallen.

A silver moon, three-quarters full, lit the scene with a clear, cold light, outlining the tall figure before her. His face was in shadow, but his eyes gleamed like a cat's.

He had obviously bathed and changed for he no longer wore his scrub suit, but a thick sweater over an open-necked shirt, and what looked like fawn cords.

Did he have a maid to attend to all his needs? Elyn wondered momentarily, and felt an odd pang at the thought. She shook herself angrily. What on earth did she care if he had an army of staff to look after him.

'I see you were about to do as I told you and get an early night,' he observed, and there was a new note in his voice.

Elyn pulled the robe more tightly round her, shivering slightly. The night air was surprisingly chill, and though she tried to deny it, Alex's unexpected appearance had thrown her off balance.

'Was there something you wanted, Dr Davidson?' Somehow it came out more stridently than she intended. He didn't appear to notice.

'Only to ensure that you have all you need and that your maid is satisfactory.'

'She's excellent,' Elyn said quickly, 'beautifully mannered and very helpful. Everything is just fine, thank you, Doctor.'

'There's no need for such formality outside the Clinic, Elyn.'

She could hear open amusement in his voice, though it was impossible to make out his expression.

'As you wish, Alex.' Though her reply was as cool and calm as the moonlight, Elyn was shaken to find herself blushing in the darkness as her lips formed his name.

'Don't forget, my office at seven-thirty in the morning, and if you oversleep, I shall personally come and wake you up, an experience you are not likely to forget.'

'I shan't oversleep,' Elyn shot back, 'but in any case, I should have thought your time was far too valuable to waste on such a trivial matter. Surely the ability to delegate is essential to someone in your position.'

'So it is,' he returned, 'but one never sends a boy to do a man's job. Goodnight Elyn, sleep well.'

Before she could utter a word, he was gone, striding away across the compound.

Quickly shutting the door Elyn leaned against it, breathing hard. He was absolutely infuriating. She walked quickly to her tiny bedroom and, flinging her robe over the sandalwood chest, she snapped out the light and climbed into bed, punching the pillow.

Elyn lay on her back, staring at the patterns formed by the moonlight on the curtains as she waited for her heartbeat to return to normal. It was a long time before sleep came.

The following morning, dressed in the white tunic and trousers Nefra had brought, Elyn entered Alex's office at twenty-five minutes past seven. He was making notes in a file and, judging by the piles of folders at various points on his desk, he had already been at work for some time.

He glanced up, frowning at the interruption. 'Ah, it's you.'

It was hardly a welcome, Elyn thought, and as a greeting it lacked warmth, but she was beginning to realise that Alex Davidson wasted little time on conventionalities.

He completed the note he was making, snapped the folder shut and stood up.

'Right, a quick ward round first. Come on.'

Holding down her irritation, Elyn followed. Why did he insist on treating her like some first-year student? However, once inside the ward the resentment that bubbled inside her at Alex's abrupt manner evaporated as she began the work she had come out here to do.

'Dr Scott, this is Sister Jehan Aldisi, you met yesterday,' Alex said as they entered the small cubicle that acted as the ward office. 'Jehan has been with me since the clinic opened nearly two years ago. She's indispensable to me.'

And I'm not, that's what you're going to such lengths to point out, Elyn fumed.

Jehan rose quickly to her feet behind her cramped desk.

'Good morning, Doctor,' she addressed Alex with respectful warmth. Then, folding her hands, she nodded politely but coolly at Elyn, seeming slightly surprised that Elyn was still on the premises.

So that's the way it's going to be, Elyn thought, well

let's see about that. She smiled pleasantly at the Egyptian nurse.

'Good morning, Sister. At my hospital in England, the medical staff relied very heavily on the sisters and their nurses for the smooth running of the wards and theatre. I'm sure that in a clinic like this, your role is even more vital.'

Elyn stepped forward and began lifting small pieces of equipment from the diagnostic tray and examining them before returning them gently to their place.

'I hope I may ask you for any help I may need over local customs regarding the other staff and patients?' She smiled as she met the older woman's eyes, 'I don't want to put my foot in it.'

Astonishment flickered across Jehan's plump face, replacing the veiled hostility in her eyes. Then she nodded, consideringly.

'I shall be happy to assist you in any way I can, Dr Scott.'

'Then may we start the round now?' Alex was clearly growing impatient.

'Of course, Doctor.' Jehan picked up three green folders from her desk and led the way out.

'How to win friends and influence people?' Alex murmured cynically to Elyn.

She shrugged and gave him a shy smile. 'It's vital that a small team work well together. I want Sister to understand that I'm trying to avoid treading on sensitive toes.' She blinked up at him, 'Anybody's,' she added lightly.

His piercing gaze sent a quiver through her. 'You're a cunning witch,' he murmured, and turned away before she had the chance to reply.

Taking the folder from Jehan, Alex approached the right side of the bed, so Elyn took the left and Jehan stationed herself at the foot.

Two other staff on the ward, a nurse and an auxiliary, were going about their duties quickly and quietly, but both were obviously surprised at Elyn's presence.

'Good morning, Hamid.' Alex addressed the patient

in Arabic, but received no reply from the young man who seemed barely conscious. His sunken eyes and pinched skin revealed the severity of his condition.

While Alex quickly scanned the chart Jehan passed him from the foot of the bed, Elyn checked the IV apparatus.

'What are you giving him?' she asked.

'Dextran and saline to counteract shock. He was admitted two days ago with crush injuries. A wall fell on him,' Alex stated, briefly.

'What about pain relief?'

'Morphine the first night, but I've switched to Papaverine because of addiction risks.'

Elyn was silent as she studied the young man whose olive skin had a greyish-yellow tinge.

'Well?' Alex prompted. 'I've given you the history, what injuries do you suspect from the visible signs?'

'Kidney damage,' Elyn replied quickly, 'he looks as though he has acute anuria.'

'Fortunately the kidneys were not ruptured, though there is severe bruising. He also has surface lacerations which I stitched yesterday.' Alex thrust the chart and folder into her unsuspecting hands. 'What treatment would you recommend, Doctor?'

Elyn looked up quickly. His face was set and ex-pressionless, but there was an odd glint in his eye.

She felt her stomach tense. Now her trial was really beginning. This was going to be like every examination she had ever taken, all rolled into one. Her place at the clinic depended upon the speed and accuracy with which she handled the questions, problems and demands hurled at her by Alex Davidson twelve hours a day for the next month.

How would she cope? There would be no allowances. If he had not already told her she would have known it from the half-impatient, half-sardonic twist to his mouth.

'Well,' he drawled impatiently.

He expected her to fail. The sudden realisation

washed over Elyn like a cold wave. He had already decided that medically she was beneath his standard. Last night's teasing must have all been part of a plan to unsettle her further.

He had told her he would ignore the fact that she was a woman, then he'd deliberately come to her bungalow at a time he knew she would be most vulnerable.

He was a cold-blooded, heartless monster. Well, he had under-estimated her. Deep in her heart, Elyn knew her broken engagement had made her question the cost of her devotion to her work. Now she knew it mattered more to her than anything else, even more than Mike, she admitted.

This post at the clinic was the realisation of a long-held dream, to provide care for people who genuinely and desperately needed it, never knowing from one day to the next what she would be called upon to deal with. Alex Davidson was not going to deprive her of the dream that had at last become reality. She would not allow it. She would fight all the way.

Summoning every bit of her concentration, Elyn took a deep breath.

She was totally unaware of Sister Jehan's puzzled glance darting from one to the other as Elyn met and held Alex's disdainful gaze, and began in a clear, calm voice to outline the recommended treatment for shock-induced kidney failure.

CHAPTER FOUR

THE next few days were a blur of activity for Elyn. Every morning work began at seven-thirty, when she checked the night reports on each occupied ward. Then she saw any new admissions and acquainted herself with their illness or injuries and the treatment Alex had prescribed.

'I'm not being gallant,' he had snapped impatiently, forestalling Elyn's request to do her share of night calls. 'I told you there would be no concessions. While I'm stuck with you, you'll do what work it suits me to give you. I prefer to deal with casualties and evaluate possible new admissions myself.' A flicker of a smile quirked his lips and was instantly gone. 'I've a strong suspicion that, left to you, this clinic would be jammed to the roof within a week.'

Elyn bit back the hot retort that sprang to her lips; she had to acknowledge he was probably right. At St Mary's she had been used, when there was doubt about a patient's condition, to admit them to the ward for observation. Here, the very limited bed space made such a move impossible, even when all her knowledge and training insisted that this course was the proper one.

So, unless the patient's condition was literally critical, they were sent home. The two paramedics plus one of the more experienced nurses did a tour of these patients daily, administering what drugs or treatment Alex prescribed on his weekly visit. They then filed a full report on their return to the clinic.

Realising that under the circumstances this was the only practical course, Elyn still found it very hard to accept, especially on occasions when it seemed to be in direct conflict with all her instincts as a doctor.

Next came ward rounds. Though the clinic had few

in-patients, those it did have were seriously ill. Two had had emergency operations and all needed constant nursing and several changes of drugs and treatment during their stay.

Since her arrival there had been no surgical emergencies, so Elyn had had no chance to observe Alex Davidson operate, nor to prove her own ability in that field. Privately she wasn't sorry. Just getting used to the heat and the new routine and coping with the work he had given her was more demanding than she would have admitted to anyone. To be forced to work alongside him in the cramped operating theatre, his dominating presence as close as her own shadow, with her surgical technique under his cold appraisal, was an experience she was glad to put off for a while longer.

The way Alex had organised things meant that officially he and Elyn had little to do with one another, except when exchanging reports. But all the time Elyn was aware of his watchful critical eyes observing every move she made. Even when he was in another part of the building she could still feel his presence. It was as though he was just behind her, looking over her shoulder, a sardonic eyebrow raised in silent query.

Sometimes this sensation of being constantly watched, added to an already demanding job, wound Elyn almost to screaming pitch. Yet though the work was tiring, she was loving every minute of it. All she wanted was the chance to do her job without Alex Davidson's contemptuous gaze pinning her down like a butterfly on a specimen board.

After ward rounds Elyn would gulp a quick cup of coffee. Jehan usually brought it herself. She had completely reversed her initial attitude and had taken Elyn under her very experienced wing.

Then it was off to the cupboard-sized laboratory to do the blood counts and test the urine samples. This was work normally done by a pathology technician.

When Alex had informed her of this extra duty, Elyn's wide-eyed start of surprise had drawn his brows together

in a frown. 'Don't tell me you've forgotten your pathology already. Damn it, you can't be that long out of
Medical School.'

At this derisive reference to her inexperience, Elyn
bristled, not realising how young she looked in her baggy
whites, with her soft chestnut curls feathering her face
and her glowing skin bare of make-up and dusted with
freckles.

'Of course I haven't forgotten, it's simply that I
haven't had much opportunity—'

'Well, you'll get plenty now,' Alex interrupted grimly.
'I thought I'd made it quite plain that we're Jacks of all
trades here. The clinic simply can't afford all the normal
hospital staff. My two senior nurses, Jehan and Magda,
take as much responsibility as a houseman would back in
England, and cope admirably.'

'Then why don't they do the path tests?' Elyn flung at
him.

'Because I can't spare them at the moment,' Alex
snapped. 'We've five desperately-ill patients on the
wards right now. All need specialling. With Jehan on
days and Magda on nights, just when are they supposed
to fit it in?'

Elyn shrank from his withering glare. She rubbed a
mark on the tiled floor with her canvas-covered toe,
wishing she hadn't spoken so hastily.

His lavish praise of the nurses and almost non-stop
criticism of her had goaded her beyond bearing. But
Elyn's innate sense of fairness forced her to admit that
Jehan and Magda had been with him a long time, and he
knew and respected their work. Whereas she had only
just arrived, unexpected, unwelcome, and as far as he
was concerned, an unknown quantity.

Elyn sighed. Why was he determined to make everything so difficult?

'When you've quite finished feeling sorry for yourself,' Alex drummed his fingers on the pile of charts in
front of him, 'perhaps you'll get along to the Lab. and
complete those tests. I'm waiting for the results.'

Elyn pressed her lips together tightly and her eyes sparked in anger as they met his hooded gaze.

'Hasn't anyone ever told you that an occasional please and thank-you would help life run much more smoothly?'

'Politeness is simply window-dressing by people who either want to make an impression or are unsure of themselves,' he said drily. 'As neither applies to me, and as I always get what I want anyway, I prefer not to waste time.'

Elyn could hardly believe her ears. She had never encountered such arrogance. She opened her mouth, a biting retort on her lips.

'The tests, Dr Scott?' His voice remained quiet, but there was an undeniable ring of steel in it.

Elyn made a superhuman effort to keep the fury that bubbled inside her out of her voice and expression. 'Do you wish to check the results, or shall I enter them directly onto the patients' charts and put the test sheets in the files?'

It would not do to reveal the extent of her dislike of him. After all, he was her superior, and even more important, he held her job in the palm of his hand, and she knew he needed only the slightest excuse to send her packing.

He studied her silently for a moment. 'Put them on the charts.' He paused, and his deep voice held a chill note of warning. 'Your accuracy had better match your confidence.'

As she returned to the wards with the test results, Elyn glanced out of the window and saw a shuffling line of men and women queueing for the outpatients clinic.

Children, ragged and barefoot, scampered about or clung to their mothers, hiding behind the long skirts as they caught sight of Elyn. As many as could sought the shade of the verandah, or even squatted beside the clinic walls. But most were left to wait in the burning glare of the sun.

About this time Elyn would swallow a hasty and very

late lunch of bread, cheese and fruit. But all too aware of the shambling line outside, the harsh murmur of voices frequently broken by the wail of a fretful child, she could not relax and enjoy it.

When, she wondered momentarily, did Alex find time to eat? There was only him to see the outpatients and the line never stopped moving. Elyn shrugged the thought away. Why should his well-being concern her in the slightest? He had made it crystal clear that his only interest lay in the patients.

After lunch she spent an hour or so in the pharmacy, acquainting herself with the drugs favoured by the clinic and preparing doses for the evening round and the following day's calls by the paramedics. There were also stock and requirement lists to update.

After checking the paramedic's reports it was time for another ward round, this time with Alex. This was a gruelling test of her knowledge and her ability to remain calm and clear-headed under his incisive questioning.

Then Elyn would stumble wearily back to her little bungalow for a refreshing shower and the meal Nefra had waiting for her.

Each evening Elyn opened her textbooks, intending to study and refresh her memory on the prevalent local diseases. But her eyelids would droop and her brain refuse to accept the words which blurred as she stared at them. Promising herself that she would study the next night, when she was sure she wouldn't be so tired, Elyn would slide between the sheets and sink into an exhausted slumber that lasted until Nefra shook her awake to begin a new day.

On the Friday morning, five days after her arrival, Elyn walked into Alex's office to collect the night reports. She had had a bad night. Despite her tiredness sleep had been elusive, and when at last it had come, it had been full of strange, disjointed dreams, all centred around the absent occupant of this office.

Elyn had woken early and Nefra had been surprised to see her already showered and dressed when she arrived to prepare breakfast. Though refreshed and surprisingly wideawake considering how little rest she'd had, Elyn still felt oddly disturbed by the dreams. There had been a haunting sweetness about them which, in the cold reality of the morning, seemed utterly ridiculous.

Of course, it was obvious *why* she'd been dreaming about him, she told herself. When someone was watching you like a hawk, waiting for you to make a mistake, and all the while making it patently clear you were only there on suffrance, you couldn't simply dismiss them from your mind when you chose.

But it really was too bad. Not only did she have to contend with his obnoxious arrogance through her working days, now he was also intruding into her private moments.

Her conscience needled. It hadn't been like that at all. The wistful sigh that shuddered from deep inside her took Elyn by surprise. Remember, her conscience insisted. Remember how his eyes, instead of glittering with impatience and contempt, were full of tenderness. Remember how his hair felt, so thick and springy, when you touched it, how it curled around your fingers as if to hold your hand. Remember his smile, a smile you've never seen, gentle, loving, curving those sensual demanding lips as they drew nearer and nearer until they touched—

The door crashed open. Elyn gasped and dropped the reports as colour flooded her face. She swung round, her heart thudding unevenly, sure he would read her thoughts as clearly as if she had spoken them aloud.

But it was not Alex who stood on the threshold.

'Dr Davidson say you come quick please,' the young nurse panted, 'he in theatre.'

Hastily picking up the reports and flinging them down on the desk, Elyn ran after the nurse. She pushed open the door of the scrub room, instinctively reluctant to go straight into the theatre in unsterile clothing and shoes.

'That you, Elyn?' Alex bellowed from inside the operating theatre.

'Yes,' Elyn shouted back.

'Scrub up as fast as you can,' he ordered. 'I've got an almost severed hand here. You'll have to assist me. Move it, girl, or we'll lose him, he's lost a lot of blood.'

'On my way.' Elyn tore off her whites and pulled on the sterile scrub suit the young nurse handed her. There was no time to think or worry about her ability to cope, about Alex watching her, about her totally confused feelings for him, or anything else at all. She had a job to do.

Bundling her hair under the green cap, she crossed to the sink and scrubbed from nails to elbows as fast as she could while taking care to be thorough. After drying them on a sterile towel, Elyn plunged her hands into the thin rubber gloves held in sterile tongs by the young nurse, then pushed open the swing doors into the operating theatre with her bottom and spun round to see Alex still in his whites.

Only they weren't white any longer. They were splattered and streaked with the blood of the young man who lay moaning on the table.

Jehan was moving swiftly between the steriliser and the instrument trolley.

'I've clamped the artery and given him a shot of morphine,' Alex said quickly. 'The tourniquet on his upper arm has just been retied so you've got ten minutes before you need to loosen it again. Get him on a dextran IV. There's no time to cross-match whole blood, so plasma will have to do. Can you manage while I scrub up?'

Elyn's glance flickered over the patient, noting the vital signs, then returned to his injury, her brain already working out procedures and techniques.

She nodded briefly and her eyes met Alex's. In that instant there were no barriers between them, no tension. They were united in the fight against death.

The doors slammed and Alex was gone, but her attention was already on the patient, now slipping into merciful unconsciousness from the effects of the morphine.

Quickly Elyn inserted a cannula into the patient's uninjured hand through which the plasma solution would drip into his veins.

'Jehan, have another bottle of dextran and one of glucose and saline standing by. We'll need them to counteract shock as well as fluid loss.' Elyn issued her instructions clearly and calmly as her mind flew ahead to all the instruments Alex would need.

'*Hanem*—the ward—Hamid's temperature is up, and there is only the junior—' Jehan's concern was evident as she placed the bottles beside the IV apparatus.

'You go on back, Jehan, I'll manage here.' Elyn's fingers flew over the instrument trolleys, selecting scissors, forceps, clamps, needles, sterile packs, towels and swabs which she laid on towels on a sterile tray.

It suddenly occurred to Elyn that Jehan had not hesitated to leave her alone, had not tactfully hinted that she wait for Alex before beginning the extremely difficult procedure of reattaching the almost severed limb.

Elyn felt a warm glow of gratitude towards the older woman, then that too was forgotten as she picked up the sterile towels and placed them around the wound in an effort to minimise the risk of infection.

Unused to seeing a theatre patient without an anesthetic mask obscuring his face and an anaesthetist sitting at his head to regulate the flow of gas and oxygen and monitor heart function and pulse rate, Elyn did a quick check herself. Then, confident that the man was indeed deeply unconscious, she loosened then retied the tourniquet and began to work.

She placed the minute stitches with infinite care, longing for the micro-surgery lasers which had recently been installed at St Mary's. Beneath her gauze mask Elyn bit her lip. It was utterly ridiculous to expect such advanced technology in a place like this.

She heard Alex's earlier words echo clearly in her mind. 'I wonder what your reaction would be, faced with

a clinic full of people and few of the facilities you appear
to despise.'

Well, this wasn't a clinic full. This was just one man,
with an injury like none Elyn had ever seen. But she
didn't have the equipment and success or failure depended, at this moment, entirely upon her and whatever
skill she possessed.

She worked on, tightly controlling the urge to hurry as
with painstaking accuracy she rejoined blood vessels,
nerves and tendons.

She was aware of Alex returning but did not look up.
Without a word she moved quickly to one side and
assumed the role of assistant and he continued where she
had left off.

The only sound was their breathing and the clink of
instruments in the metal dishes. She anticipated each
move and had the necessary clamp, swab or needle
ready before he needed to ask.

His gloved hands moved with the deftness and preci-
sion of a natural surgeon. Elyn realised, after only a few
seconds, that had he stayed in England or America he
would have been famous and could have commanded
astronomical fees, had he so wished.

What then was he doing out here? A talent such as his
was unique. Why did he choose to bury it in a tiny desert
clinic? Then even those thoughts faded as she concentrated on her task.

As the wound was finally closed Elyn noticed Alex
take great care to ensure that the edges met cleanly.
There must be no gathering, no dragging of the skin, or
ugly, painful scarring would result, and out here, plastic
surgery to repair the results of such carelessness was out
of the question.

Then it was finished. Elyn dropped the last swab into
the bucket and straightened up, wincing a little at the
stiffness in her back and shoulders. A glance at the
electric clock on the wall made her blink in amazement.
They had been bent over the unconscious man for two
hours.

Alex pushed the instrument tray aside. 'Call Jehan, he's ready for the ward,' he said quietly and, turning away, pushed open the doors and walked out of the theatre.

Disappointment speared Elyn as she stared after him. That was all? She had hoped—just a word—some acknowledgement of the challenge they had faced together, and overcome.

She shook her head, exasperated with herself. Of course he would not bother with such a thing. It was no more than he expected, no, demanded of his staff. She was only doing her job. Why on earth should she expect praise for it? He'd soon make it clear if she put a foot wrong. Besides, she didn't even like him, so why should his personal opinions concern her in the least?

Elyn called Jehan and between them the young man was soon in bed in a fresh hospital gown. The thick bandages were starkly white against his swarthy skin, and the thin rubber tube strapped to his other hand steadily dripped life-giving fluid from the suspended bottle into his unconscious body.

When he was settled Elyn left the ward to go back to the scrub room to wash and change. As she reached the door and pushed it open, Alex's voice echoed in the passage, making her jump.

'When you're ready, come to my office.'

Elyn spun round, but the office door swung shut and she was alone. She shrugged, stretching her shoulders to ease the slight tension that remained.

Her first operation in the clinic. Was that what he wanted to see her about? Was he going to criticise her technique, or the fact that she'd sent Jehan back to the ward? Elyn took a deep breath. Don't be silly, she admonished herself, you did all right in there, you know you did.

She couldn't suppress a small smile. She had helped to make someone whole again. It was a marvellous feeling. Her knowledge and training had helped save a man's life. It filled her with joy, pride and humility all at the same time. There was no more rewarding job in the world, of that she was certain.

Drying her hands and face, Elyn pushed her towel and scrub suit into the dirty-linen basket and dressed once again in her whites. She pulled a comb through her hair and went out into the corridor.

How different it had been from St Mary's, she mused as she walked along to Alex's office. There, when she had assisted in theatre, there had been a consultant surgeon, a registrar, a senior houseman and herself, plus two theatre nurses, a scrub nurse and a 'dirty' nurse, as well as porters to bring the patient to and from the theatre.

Would you go back? The question taunted her. Her answer, surprising her with its force, was an immediate and unequivocal no. She had no time to wonder at her own reaction.

Opening Alex's door, she walked in, a faint pinkness warming her cheeks as she remembered her thoughts the first time she had entered his office that morning.

Alex was sitting at his desk, swinging his chair gently to and fro as he studied the contents of the folder open before him. He had washed and changed into clean whites and looked as fresh and relaxed as if he'd just got out of bed instead of completing a long and tricky operation only minutes before.

He made no acknowledgement of her presence and Elyn felt irritation begin to needle. Nothing had changed. It was as though the last two hours, the unspoken understanding and almost telepathic awareness, had never happened. Unreasoning disappointment flooded through her.

'You wished to see me?' her tone was more abrupt than she had intended.

He looked up and stopped swinging the chair. 'Ah, Elyn,' he said coolly, and instead of returning his gaze to the paperwork as he normally did, he continued to watch her with an enigmatic expression that immediately had Elyn on the defensive.

Had something gone wrong? Had she made a mistake? A blood count? A drug dose? Why didn't he say something instead of simply staring at her as though she were something interesting on a microscope slide.

'Why so nervous, Elyn?' he mocked. She swallowed the sudden dryness in her throat. Why *did* he unnerve her like this? He was like some large predatory animal, a tiger, playing with its victim before delivering the final stunning blow.

'Cat got your tongue?' Alex murmured deep in his throat.

Yet again Elyn had the uncanny feeling he could read her thoughts. She coloured rosily and her eyes flashed.

'Your attitude doesn't exactly inspire confidence, Dr Davidson.'

'Is that why we're so formal today?' He seemed to be laughing. 'I thought I told you to call me Alex.'

'And I thought that only applied when we were off duty, and as I never see you off duty—' Elyn shrugged dismissively.

'Is that a complaint, Elyn? Do you feel neglected?' His green eyes probed hers, making her uncomfortably aware of the forcefulness of his personality, his powerful masculinity.

'Of course not,' she retorted hotly. The ego of the man! As if she would want to see any more of him that she absolutely had to.

'I did warn you about conditions out here.' Alex's eyes held hers and she couldn't look away. 'If you need flocks of young men hovering around you then you've come to the wrong place.'

'I don't—I've never—I mean—' Elyn was almost speechless with anger.

'Then—what?' His voice was a mere rumble and his eyes challenging. Elyn was suddenly aware of a new element in the tension between them.

'That patient—in theatre—' she burst out.

'What about him?' Alex seemed surprised.

Elyn's thoughts raced. She couldn't deliberately seek

his approval, she simply couldn't. It would be like begging for crumbs and she had too much pride for that.

'How—how did he get that dreadful wound?' she managed at last.

'I haven't got the full story yet myself,' Alex frowned, 'but I gather he was caught stealing.'

'And that was his punishment?' Elyn gasped, horrified.

'It is Koranic law. It was not the first time and he was seen by three witnesses, necessary conditions before the law can be invoked.'

'Yes, but—' Elyn began, then stopped, not because of Alex's warning frown, but because she was a stranger in this land and had no right to pass judgment on a situation she knew nothing about.

'You were about to say?' Alex prompted drily.

Elyn shook her head. 'Nothing. It seems barbaric,' she shuddered, 'but I'm an outsider. Perhaps some of our laws would be incomprehensible to the people here.' She shrugged and turned away.

'Just a moment, I haven't finished with you yet,' Alex said silkily.

Elyn turned round slowly to face him.

'You'll be coming with me to Kharga this afternoon.' His face was expressionless.

'Me?' Elyn was taken completely by surprise. 'What for?' Suddenly she was wary. 'Is this some roundabout way of getting rid of me? The month isn't up yet, I haven't had—'

'What a suspicious little thing you are,' he interrupted, an amused grin playing at the corners of his mouth. 'No, I'm not sending you away—for the moment,' he added darkly. 'I'm going to the hospital at Kharga for supplies. They come in by rail and truck once a month and we have to collect ours from there. As I have no clinic this afternoon, and you have finished in the pharmacy, I thought you might like a change of scene.'

Elyn could hardly believe her ears. He sounded

almost friendly. There must be something wrong. This wasn't the Alex Davidson she knew, and though she didn't like the other one, at least she was used to him.

Her face must have mirrored her thoughts for he stood up abruptly, exasperation creasing his forehead.

'Look, I've no devious scheme up my sleeve. I'm not planning to dump you in the desert, or hurl you screaming onto a train.'

Elyn looked down at the floor quickly.

'As a matter of fact,' he went on with exaggerated patience, 'the train left two days ago. Does that put your mind at rest?'

'I wasn't—I mean, I didn't—' Elyn spluttered.

'And spare me any lies,' Alex said drily, leaning over the desk towards her. 'You're transparent, Elyn.' He stood upright once more and began sorting some papers on his desk, his whole attention seemingly concentrated on them. 'I want you with me to learn the system. It's just possible that sometime you might have to do the job instead of me. Surely you remember the law?'

'Law?' Elyn repeated vaguely.

'Yes,' he was terse. 'Drugs on the Schedule IV Poisons and Dangerous Drugs Act lists can only be released on a doctor's signature. A lot of use you'll be if you've no idea where to go, who to see or what to get.'

Elyn bit her lip. What a prize idiot he must think her. Yet he could hardly blame her for jumping to conclusions. Then the full meaning of his words sunk in.

'You mean—you're letting me stay? You're satisfied with my work—?'

Elyn could have bitten her tongue off. She hadn't meant to say it, the words had slipped out. Blushing furiously, she stared at the floor, trying frantically to think of something to say to cover her gaffe. She closed her eyes, anticipating his scathing retort.

'Let's just say, you aren't quite as much of a handicap as I had expected you to be.'

Even without looking she could sense his eyes on her.

'Thank you,' she murmured acidly.

'But now perhaps a ward round?' His acid matched her own. 'There's still the whole of the morning's work to get through and we're already running over two hours late.'

Elyn jumped as if she'd been stung. 'Of course, Doctor,' she replied crisply and started for the door.

'Meet me by the gate at two o'clock.' Tossing the words over his shoulder Alex walked out of the office and into the ward, leaving Elyn staring after him.

There were several questions she would have liked to ask him. What should she wear? Was she expected to go in hospital whites as the trip was on hospital business? Would they have time to go into the town? Should she take any money? But his sudden lapse into mild pleasantness was obviously over and regretted. His leave-taking had been much more the man she knew and intensely disliked.

Shrugging off the frustration he seemed inevitably to arouse in her, Elyn walked briskly out of the office to begin her own morning's work.

Refusing coffee, and swallowing a hasty lunch only because Jehan insisted, Elyn managed to complete all her duties, even her paperwork, leaving herself just ten minutes to get ready.

She raced back to her bungalow, the sweat breaking out on her like dew as she crossed the compound to her front door.

Tearing off her clothes she tossed them into a corner and stepped quickly under the shower. The cool water refreshed and revitalised her. She quickly towelled dry and as she liberally sprinkled on talcum powder, Elyn found herself viewing the trip with very mixed feelings.

What on earth would they talk about, that hard arrogant man and herself? What if he didn't want to talk at all? Elyn's stomach tightened with tension. It would be awful. Just the two of them in the confined cab of a Land Rover. Herself sitting next to a man who disturbed her more than any man she had ever known, a man she disliked with an intensity that shocked her, yet dreamed about—

A little gasp escaped her lips and she flung the towel over the rail and pulled on fresh bra and pants. In a gesture of defiance she kicked the hospital suit aside, selecting instead a butter-yellow cotton tee-shirt and matching cotton trousers. After raking a comb through her still-damp curls and adding a touch of lip-stick for her ego's sake, she was ready.

As she reached the door it occurred to her that he hadn't told her what time they'd be back. But as it was business and not pleasure, he'd probably want to return to the clinic as quickly as possible. No need then for a sweater, they'd be back long before the temperature dropped at sundown.

Slamming the door shut, she hurried across the compound to the main gate. The scent of the flowers wafted across to her, their colours vivid and lush against the sandy soil and the azure canopy of sky.

'At last,' Alex muttered, revving the engine impatiently as Elyn clambered in and shut the door. A quick glance at her watch told her it was only three minutes after two.

'I'm sorry I'm late,' she began breathlessly, 'but—'

'I'm not interested in your excuses,' he snapped, swinging the Land Rover out of the compound and along the track. Among the palm trees little houses were scattered, their white walls gleaming in the brilliant sunshine and their flat roofs reminding Elyn of upturned boxes or a child's building bricks.

The oasis seemed deserted, but once or twice she caught a glimpse of a black-swathed figure. Chickens and geese squawked and flapped out of their way as the Land Rover's engine shattered the sultry silence. Fawn dust rose in a cloud behind them, then settled over their tracks, obliterating them as though they had never been.

'Then I'll waste neither my breath nor your time,' Elyn retorted. 'However, it might interest you to know that Hamid's blood sodium and potassium levels have stabilised, and his kidneys began functioning normally just after one-fifteen.'

Alex glanced at her. 'What have you done about the IVs?'

'Taken him off saline, he can have salt by mouth if his urine output depletes the blood level again. But I've kept him on glucose until he starts eating.'

'Good,' Alex nodded briefly, and stared ahead through the windscreen as they bumped along the track.

And that's as much as I'll get out of him, Elyn thought furiously. The fight to pull Hamid through the crisis caused by his damaged kidneys had been a very difficult one. Each day that had passed without any stabilisation in his condition had brought him nearer to death.

Elyn had taken a special interest in his case, partly because he was the patient just coming out of the operating theatre at the moment of her arrival, and then because Jehan had told her that he had been married only a few weeks.

Elyn had seen his wife, a plump, sloe-eyed girl, scarcely more than a child herself, but heavily veiled as befitted a modest married woman. She came twice each day to sit with her husband, whispering softly to him, her gaze never leaving his face, though he was unconscious and showed no sign of hearing her. Not once did she touch him, a fact that Elyn found strange until Jehan explained that demonstrations of affection between men and women in public were frowned upon.

'Even if they are married,' Jehan had said, 'such behaviour is for the privacy of home, not for public gaze.'

Busy in the office one day, Elyn had glimpsed the girl's arrival and found her attention caught. The girl's eyes were red and swollen from crying, but not once did a tear fall while she was by her husband's side. Elyn could almost feel the girl willing her man to fight, to get better and return to her and the little house Jehan had told Elyn he'd built with his own hands.

A strange yearning gripped her. What was it like to

love someone with such intensity, and to be loved the same way in return? How would it feel to be the centre of someone's world, the reason they wanted to go on living?

'The sooner we can discharge him, the better,' Alex muttered, breaking into her musing.

'Why?' Elyn was startled. She braced herself with her arms to prevent herself being flung against either Alex or the door, as the Land Rover rattled out of the green coolness of the oasis and up the rutted, pot-holed track which ran along the valley.

'We're going to need every bed we've got,' he said grimly.

Elyn was bewildered. 'What do you mean? How do you know?'

Alex's jaw was set and Elyn could sense barely-controlled rage in every tense muscle of his body.

'When Mohammed and Salah made their reports this morning, they informed me that one of the main irrigation channels I'd insisted two weeks ago should be drained and treated with pesticide, is still being used.'

'Will two weeks make a lot of difference?' Elyn ventured, half expecting him to blow her head off, yet still not understanding the reason for his anger. 'I mean, if it's done soon—'

'It will still be too late,' he growled. '*Cercariae*, *Doctor* Scott,' the emphasis was heavy, 'parasites which escape from their host, the freshwater snail, and penetrate human skin. Do you know what I'm talking about?' He flung the words at her, taking his eyes from the track long enough to see horrified comprehension dawn on Elyn's face.

'Bilharzia?' she murmured.

He nodded abruptly.

'Heavy primary infection?'

He nodded again.

'How many?' Elyn asked.

'God knows,' he shrugged wearily. 'I'm already treating three-quarters of the local population for bilharzia.

Mostly the primary infection has been light and they've responded quickly to treatment. But keeping them out of infected water has been an uphill struggle.'

'I suppose—if it's their livelihood—' Elyn shrugged helplessly.

'I know,' he agreed, surprising her. 'If they don't work, they starve. If they do work in infected water, they could die. Not an easy choice for them, is it?' He sighed wearily. 'Perhaps if enough of them become acutely ill this time, they'll drain the damn channel and treat it. In the meantime, I'll be faced with some difficult choices of my own.'

He intercepted her condemning glance, and his mouth twisted in a sardonic grin. 'I was right, you are transparent, Elyn. I can see accusation written all over your face. You'd have the clinic packed to the doors, despite our lack of facilities and staff.' He shook his head slowly. 'What on earth are you doing out here in the desert, Elyn Scott? Why aren't you back home in England with a husband and a houseful of children upon whom to lavish your over-abundant milk-of-human-kindness?'

'Why you, you pompous—' Elyn exploded. 'How dare you be so patronising? Just because I care—'

'And I don't?' he snarled, 'is that what you're implying? Do you think you have a monopoly on caring? Don't you have the sense to realise that judgments based on emotion are irrational and dangerous?'

His face was thunderous and Elyn felt the force of his anger directed at her like a physical blow. She flinched.

'Do you think it's easy, choosing who to admit to the clinic and who to turn away, knowing all too often it could mean the difference between life and death?' He snorted in disgust and turned his attention to the track which wound up out of the widening valley onto the hilly plateau.

'We can't all play God,' Elyn cried wildly, shaken by his ferocious attack on her. She was also, suddenly, uncomfortably aware of the colossal pressures upon him. Pressures she had only glimpsed, and which he usually handled with such ease and efficiency she was hardly aware of their existence. But that still didn't excuse his behaviour towards her.

'I'm not saying yours is an easy position,' Elyn blurted, 'but neither is mine. All day I'm seeing desperately ill people and I can't forget that there are dozens more who need the help and treatment we could provide if only we had more—' she shrugged helplessly, 'more of everything.'

Her first wild rage was beginning to subside and she felt curiously weak and near to tears. Struggling to disguise the tremor in her voice, she threw the words at him, 'And you certainly don't help.'

'Oh? Why?' He had himself completely under control once more. The sardonic mask was back in place and an amused grin lifted one corner of his mouth. 'Because I dared to suggest you should be married, with children?'

'No—yes—' Why did he confuse her so?

'Is that such an insult then?' he mocked, 'surely it's a woman's natural role?'

'That may be so,' Elyn retorted, 'but it doesn't preclude her from wanting to do something else with her life.'

'Best of both worlds?'

His derision stung. 'Why not?' she flared, 'men do, and no-one thinks that strange. In fact, a successful man is considered odd if he doesn't have a wife and children sitting at home waiting for him.'

Elyn took a deep breath. 'For your information, Dr Davidson, I'm a perfectly normal woman,' Elyn knew her tongue was running away with her, but she was so infuriated she could not stop. 'I hope to marry one day, and have children, but until I do, I intend to go on doing the job I love, which I've trained long and hard for,' she drew in a shaky breath then plunged recklessly on, 'and which despite your high-handed, overbearing, hypercritical attitude, I know I'm good at!'

She turned her head away from him and stared out of the window, opening her eyes very wide so that the tears which threatened would not actually spill over and fall. That would be too awful. He'd probably make some scathing remark about her resorting to feminine tricks to win his sympathy. Well, she wasn't. She hated the way her emotions ran so near the surface. She didn't want his sympathy. All she wanted, all she had ever wanted, was his professional respect, his acknowledgement of her ability as a doctor. Had she been a man, she'd have had it within hours of her arrival.

It was he who was the cause of all the problems between them. He was everything she had said, and worse. And now she had made him angry again. Well, what if she had? He could hardly throw her out in the middle of the desert.

No, a small voice reminded her, but he could refuse to let you return. He could leave you at Kharga and send your things on, thereby ridding himself of your unexpected and unwelcome presence.

If he chose to do that there was nothing she could do. His word was law. He had warned her and she had chosen to ignore him. He was her superior and she had been unforgivably rude. Elyn clenched her fists in her lap. Maybe he had deserved it, but what was it going to cost her?

'So, the kitten has sharp claws,' he murmured thoughtfully.

'I—I—' Elyn began.

'An apology?' he interrupted her with a mocking smile. 'If you meant what you said, and from the fervour in your voice I'd say you did, then the apology would be a lie. If you didn't mean it, the apology is too late.'

Too late. Despite the heat, Elyn shivered. No other words contained so much sadness and regret. She had only herself to blame. If she could only take back her hasty words. Not that they hadn't been thoroughly deserved. But what about her job?

'Look over there, Elyn.'

The sound of his voice, so calm and emotionless

compared with her own chaotic thoughts, startled her out of her reverie. Automatically she followed his pointing finger, consciously seeing her surroundings for the first time in several minutes.

The plateau had levelled out and the track was now running through the middle of a vast area under intensive cultivation. Elyn noticed, dotted about at odd intervals, complicated structures of pipes and valves a few feet high, that gleamed metallically in the brilliant sunlight.

'What are those?' she asked, scarcely able to believe her eyes. Huge squares of different crops, barley, beans, onions and flax, formed a colossal patchwork over the plateau. Along the irrigation channels and among the crops men and women worked, like ants.

'They are the well heads,' Alex explained without a trace of mockery. 'They tap the underground water that has made all this possible.'

'It's fantastic,' Elyn breathed, totally forgetting in her excitement her dislike of the man beside her. 'All this richness, right out here in the middle of the desert, it's unbelievable. What's that big area of green, over there?'

Alex slowed the Land Rover and looked across to where Elyn pointed out of the window, sliding his arm along the back of the seat while leaning towards her for a clearer view.

Elyn's breath caught in her throat at his sudden nearness. She felt the slow burn of awareness tingle through her and silently railed at her body's betrayal. Please don't let him notice, she prayed.

'That's bersim,' Alex said, seemingly oblivious of Elyn's immobility. 'Alexandrian clover, to feed livestock, goats, donkeys, and sheep. I'm told it's only used as a rotation crop to fix the nitrogen in the soil. It doesn't make very good hay.'

The Land Rover had rolled to a stop. Elyn stared out of her side window, not seeing a thing, aware only of the man almost touching her, the muscular contours of his chest and shoulders straining his thin shirt, for he too had changed out of hospital clothing.

His breath was warm on her neck. Elyn's heart pounded so loudly she was terrified he would hear it. Why? Why? The question spun crazily in her brain.

Mike had never affected her like this. They had been engaged for two years, she had thought she loved him, thought he stirred her. But never, even in their most intimate moments, had she plunged into the tumult of emotional and physical awareness that she experienced in Alex Davidson's presence. And she wasn't in love with *him*. She didn't even like him. In fact he was the most infuriating, frustrating, detestable man she had ever had the misfortune to meet.

'Are you all right, Elyn?'

Elyn started. He actually sounded concerned.

'Yes—yes.' She swallowed quickly, willing her voice to remain cool and calm.

'You look a bit feverish to me, high colour, over-bright eyes.'

Still that note of concern. It sounded almost genuine, but Elyn wasn't fooled. This was just another ploy, another trick to prove her unfit to work in desert conditions, another excuse to get rid of her.

His fingers rested lightly on her neck for a moment, then trailed across her throat to rest on the sunkissed skin of her cheek.

With a gasp Elyn leapt away from him, feeling the inprint of his touch like a fiery brand as she tingled with shock.

'I'm—I'm all right,' she stammered breathlessly, not daring to meet his eyes. 'It's just the heat in here—the metal, it's so hot—'

She was babbling. She must stop it at once or he'd have good reason to believe there was something wrong with her.

'Oh look,' she said hastily, 'there's someone over by that well-head. It looks like Tim. Shall we go and say hello?' Elyn put her hand on the door.

'No.' It was a command and a refusal, delivered so tersely that Elyn blinked in surprise as she glanced sideways at Alex.

Sliding back into the driving seat he slammed the engine in gear and the Land Rover roared forward with a jerk that jolted Elyn backwards, bumping her head.

'It wouldn't have taken long,' she said, rubbing the bump, 'and he is a friend.'

'Really?', Alex's voice was cold and he raised one eyebrow in sarcastic query. 'How long have you known him?'

'Only a couple of days, well—not even that really, but—'

'But you know him well enough to call him a friend.' Alex's voice dripped scorn.

'He was pleasant and helpful,' Elyn protested, driven to defend Tim though the memory of his behaviour at the inn prodded her uncomfortably.

'For which he was amply rewarded, no doubt.'

'I don't know what you mean.' What exactly was he implying? Elyn felt anger stirring, and at the same time a sense of danger.

'Come on, Elyn,' Alex's derision was open. 'You're not a child. A chap like Tim Preston doesn't do favours for nothing.'

Elyn was growing angrier by the minute. 'I don't know what you're talking about, and I don't think I want to know. Someone as cynical as you wouldn't recognise friendship if it was offered.' Elyn's eyes flashed blue fire as she raged at him. 'I don't know what gave you such a low opinion of your fellow human-beings, but I think you're to be pitied.'

Alex's voice was pure ice. 'Oh, you do. Well, that is something we'll discuss at a later date. In the meantime, you are to stay away from Preston.'

'What?' Elyn gasped. 'Just who do you think you are to tell me who I can and can't—'

'I'm your employer—at the moment,' he said deliberately. The warning was unmistakable. 'And as such I have every intention of keeping you out of a situation which could interfere with your ability to do your job to my satisfaction.' The ice seemed to have melted, leaving only amusement in his tone.

'But that's blackmail,' Elyn whispered, appalled by his arrogance. She faced him defiantly. 'Do I assume then that you intend to choose my friends for me? Am I allowed any at all? Just why should I let you?'

His reply was swift and brutal. 'Because you obviously lack judgment.'

'How dare you! You don't—'

'The subject is closed, Elyn,' he snapped. She opened her mouth in protest. 'Closed, I said,' he repeated with chilling finality.

A few moments later they pulled into the palm-shaded grounds of Kharga Hospital and Elyn had no choice but to thrust her bitterly angry thoughts from her mind.

She was here as part of her job and that took precedence over everything, even her hatred of the tall, broad-shouldered man who strode purposefully beside her. His ruthless determination was hidden behind an enigmatic smile as he pushed open the door and stood aside to allow her through.

CHAPTER FIVE

As THE Land Rover roared away from the hospital, its precious load of drugs and supplies having been stacked under Alex's lynx-eyed supervision, Elyn shot him a tentative glance. 'We're going straight back?'

He nodded briefly and she tried to shrug off her disappointment. She would have loved to look around the small, ancient town and explore the souk, the heart of the oasis, where leather and cloth, silver jewellery and copper lamps, furniture, fruit and spices were bought and sold.

Elyn wanted to buy gifts for her father and Aunt Connie, something typical of the place in which she was living. She sighed ruefully. It was just as well you couldn't gift-wrap heat, sand, dust and tiredness. She wondered momentarily if she would get the chance to do shopping or exploring of any kind before her six months contract was up. Life at the clinic was undoubtedly hectic. She certainly didn't have the problem of too much time on her hands.

Even the last hour, while a welcome change from clinic routine, had been something of an ordeal.

Despite the undoubted politeness of all the staff to whom she had been introduced, there had been no escaping their surprise and curiosity. Elyn had begun to expect the slight widening of the eyes followed by a startled glance at Alex. Then her outstretched hand would be briefly shaken and conventional greetings exchanged, and all the time she could feel the unspoken question hovering in the air, what on earth was she doing here?

While Elyn's self-consciousness grew, heightening her colour and making her feel like some rather odd medical specimen, Alex remained aloof and expressionless, according her the exact amount of professional courtesy due, while he explained all the necessary details of the transactions with his customary brisk efficiency.

If the administrator, the chief physician, his registrar, the surgical registrar and the pharmacist had hoped or expected Alex would reveal his true feelings about her presence among them, they hid their disappointment well. Yet, from their almost tangible curiosity, Elyn knew that Alex must have made it as clear to them as he had to her that a female doctor was about as welcome at his clinic as the plague.

'I'm aware you've had no time off, since your arrival,' Alex broke into her thoughts, and again she had the uncanny feeling that he could read her mind, 'and I had intended to take you into the souk. There are some interesting early Christian tombs not far from here—' he broke off, waving a dismissive hand. 'You're probably not interested in archaeology.'

'I don't know a lot about it, but I *am* interested,' Elyn corrected him firmly, 'historically this must be the most fascinating country in the world—' She caught her breath.

Alex was driving the Land Rover hard, spinning the wheel to avoid the roughest parts of the track as they hurtled through the rich fertile fields and out once more onto the plateau. Elyn was thrown about and jolted unmercifully. It was dreadfully uncomfortable and, combined with the heat, was beginning to make her feel queasy.

'Please,' she gasped, after a particularly violent swerve had thrown her against the door, leaving her arm and shoulder numb. 'Could you slow down a bit. Why the rush? And why couldn't we have stayed a little longer in Kharga?'

He didn't answer her directly. 'Look out of your window,' he ordered, slowing down. Elyn looked. 'Tell me what you see,' he demanded.

Elyn screwed up her eyes in effort. 'Nothing,' she said

slowly. 'I can't see much at all. Even the sun seems to be blurred and the air is full of dust.' She swivelled round on the seat to stare at Alex as with a sudden movement and a grim sigh he pulled the Land Rover off the track and into the lee of a small stony hill.

'What are you doing? Why have we stopped?' Elyn was more puzzled than alarmed.

'Sandstorm,' Alex replied succinctly. 'That's why the rush and why we didn't do any sight-seeing. Just before we left the hospital Dr Selim told me that a warning message had been received from the survey station to the south-west of Kharga. I was hoping we could get back to Khalifa before it hit us, but we aren't going to make it.'

Elyn stared at him for a few seconds, not wanting to believe what she had heard, then swung round to look out of the window again.

The sky, instead of the intense blue she now took for granted, was a dirty fawn colour, through which a crimson sun glowered balefully in the thickening air. The heat was even more oppressive now they had stopped moving. But that was not the only reason for the perspiration that beaded Elyn's forehead, dampening her hair into spiky curls, and forming damp patches on her thin tee-shirt. Fear, like icy water, trickled down her spine.

'If you knew it was coming, why didn't we stay in Kharga and wait for it to pass?' Elyn demanded, nervousness giving her voice an edge.

'Because, my dear Elyn, sandstorms can last for minutes or for days, and as Khalifa Clinic requires my presence, plus these supplies, to function at all, I could hardly hang about in Kharga when there was a chance we might have made it home.'

He sounded so sensible, so reasonable, as he half-turned in his seat, resting one arm on the steering wheel and the other along the back of Elyn's seat.

Elyn could feel the tension twisting her stomach into a knot. 'But we can't just sit here and do nothing.' She clenched her fingers together so tightly, her knuckles gleamed white.

Alex's glance took in Elyn's clasped hands, her pale face and wide eyes, and a puzzled frown creased his forehead.

'What do you suggest?' he asked with unexpected gentleness. 'It might well be over in half an hour or so.'

'But you said they sometimes last for—for days,' Elyn whispered.

'It has been known,' he admitted, 'but not all that often. Usually it's an hour or two at the most.' Then, reaching beneath the seat, he pulled out a vacuum jug and a sealed container of paper cups. He broke open the pack and balanced two cups on the flat surface above the dash-board. Pouring iced orange juice into the cups he recorked the jug and passed one cup to Elyn.

'Have a drink and try to relax. I assure you, you're quite safe in here.'

Elyn's hand trembled as she took the cup and raised it to her lips. She swallowed and the cold juice was like nectar to her parched throat. She quickly gulped down the rest.

A gust of wind buffetted the Land Rover, hurling sand against the metal and glass with a soft hiss. Elyn's fingers tightened convulsively, crushing the paper cup.

The light was fading fast as the fawn dust and sand whirled about them, driven by a screaming wind that hit them with the suddenness and strength of an express train.

Elyn gasped and a small sob escaped her lips, lips taut and dry with fear. She clapped her hands over her ears to try and shut out the sound. The air in the cab was growing hotter and more difficult to breathe as dust particles penetrated every crack and crevice.

The wind was a living force smashing against the Land Rover, despite the protection of the hill. The sun vanished and only a faint duskiness remained. Elyn felt panic bubbling within her and bit her lips to hold back the scream that was perilously near.

Alex was studying her closely in the dim light. 'Elyn, what's the matter? What are you afraid of?' He sounded perplexed and even in her terror Elyn heard that same note of concern she had detected earlier.

She thought of denying the truth, of trying to hide her weakness, and laugh off her fear and misery. But another gust of wind slammed into the Land Rover, threatening to crush the metal like tissue paper, causing the vehicle to shudder and robbing Elyn of all her proud intentions.

She swallowed, fighting to stay calm. 'I—I suffer from claustrophobia,' she forced the words out, trying with every ounce of strength to ignore the noise, the darkness and the stifling heat. Her fear was illogical, she knew that, but she couldn't overcome it. She had tried, oh how she had tried.

'I'm all right in small, confined places, as long as it's light—' she faltered, 'but this is like being sealed inside a tin can.' She began to gasp. 'I can't stay in here, I've got to get out,' she cried desperately. 'I can't breathe, there's no air left.' Her voice rose to a thin scream as she hurled herself against the door, scrabbling for the handle.

Alex seized her, his hands on her shoulders, firmly drawing her away from the door.

'If you go out there, you'll suffocate,' he said sharply. 'This is the only safe place, Elyn. You must stay inside.' He drew her towards him, his voice becoming gentler.

'There's nothing to fear. The darkness is only temporary. Once the sandstorm passes it will be light again. Nothing will have changed.'

His arms enfolded her, pressing her against his chest, her head rested in the hollow between his neck and shoulder. And suddenly, inexplicably, she felt safe.

Part of her protested. She was mad. He was no friend of hers. He was trying to lull her into a false sense of security. Sooner or later he would use this against her. A desert doctor afraid of a sandstorm? He would never let her forget that. But the sensation of his arms around her was undeniably comforting. She could feel the mind-numbing fear draining away, leaving her limp and shaken. She could hear his heartbeat, strong, regular, reassuring.

Unconsciously, like a child, Elyn nestled closer. She heard his sudden soft intake of breath, but it didn't register.

Outside, sand and wind boiled around them like some witch's cauldron. The spitting hiss of sand, blasting against the metal shell protecting them, underlay the high-pitched keening of a wind that shrieked like souls in torment.

Gradually Elyn became aware of a change in Alex. His arms no longer rested loosely about her. Tension corded his muscles and as he moved his chin away from where it rested against her head, he raised his hand, spreading his fingers around her throat and neck. He tilted her chin with his thumb.

Elyn's hazy cocoon of comfort and security was ripped aside, as in a blinding flash of clarity she realised he was going to kiss her.

She went rigid, but before she could push him away, his dark head came down and she heard him murmur her name before his lips descended on hers.

For a split second she couldn't move, then she began to struggle.

His mouth bore down on hers, crushing her lips, forcing them apart, seeking, demanding. Elyn made desperate efforts to free herself, but against his strength she had no chance.

One of his arms imprisoned her, crushing her painfully against his chest. The heat of their bodies burned through the thin shirts and his heart-beat thudded against her breast. His other hand held her head, and Elyn knew his strength was such that he could snap her neck like a twig.

Then, suddenly, the fight was over. Against her will her body began to respond. The blood drummed in her veins and her limbs became heavy and languorous. Her lips trembled against his, growing soft and warm as the tip of his exploring tongue sent a white-hot flame shooting through her body.

Sensing the change in her, a soft animal sound came from deep in Alex's throat. Her body seemed to melt into him. She was adrift on an ocean of sensuality, pounded by waves of desire so powerful, they took her breath away.

His hand left her neck to run through her chestnut curls, then tightened on them, pulling her head back as he tore his mouth from hers and rained kisses on her eyes, cheeks and throat, each one a brand on her skin, together a trail of fire revealing the truth as it burned into her innermost soul.

She had assumed the animosity, the anger, the electric tension between them was due to a clash of personalities, a strong mutual dislike. But it was none of those things. She had deluded herself. It wasn't hatred she felt for Alex Davidson. She had fallen deeply, irrevocably in love with him.

His kiss had pierced her armour of self-deception, and she saw clearly for the first time what she had refused to acknowledge, even to herself. From that moment in Cairo Airport when he had lectured her on her stupidity, she had been lost. With the realisation came despair. It spread like ice-water through her fevered body and brought her crashing back to harsh reality.

To love him was hopeless. Alex Davidson could never return her feelings. He only tolerated her because of the difficulties involved in replacing her. He had not wanted her here in the first place and had done all in his power to prove her unsuitable for the job. What little praise he had given she had virtually asked for. As far as he was concerned she was nothing more than an unwelcome guest, to be tolerated until her contract was up, when she would be replaced with the utmost speed.

These kisses meant nothing to him—how could they when she meant nothing? It had probably been the only way he could control her hysterical outburst without slapping her face.

Alex Davidson was totally male, strong, virile, powerful. Stuck in a Land Rover with a terrified female who had clung like a limpet, what other reaction could she have expected?

A crimson blush of shame scalded Elyn from her toes to the roots of her hair. What on earth would he think of her? Never before had she experienced such shatteringly powerful feelings as those moments in his arms. But he must never know the truth.

She could not bear to imagine his contempt, his icy scorn, or worse still, his pity, should he guess she was in love with him. From now on she was going to need every ounce of self-control. Thank goodness she had an excuse for what had just occurred.

Sensing the change in her, Alex lifted his lips from the soft skin of her throat. 'Elyn?' he murmured hoarsely.

Elyn seized the opportunity to push herself upright, though her heart tore as the contact between them was severed.

'I'm sorry,' she whispered, her heart thumping wildly as she held herself rigidly away from him, knowing that if he touched her she would betray herself.

'It's such a stupid thing. I know there's nothing to be afraid of, but ever since I got trapped in a wardrobe when I was three, I've had this ridiculous fear of darkness in confined spaces. Please forgive me.'

His brows drew together in a puzzled frown. 'Forgive you? What for?'

'For behaving so childishly.' She flashed him a bright smile. 'But I'm fine now,' she assured him airily. 'It's getting lighter. The sandstorm must be blowing over, just as you said it would. We should be able to start back for Khalifa soon.'

Elyn sensed her brittle chatter shattering the precious moments into a million fragments. She wanted to weep. But she had to convince him that nothing particularly important or out of the ordinary had happened between them. She could not know that she was succeeding only too well. Desolation filled her heart with a pain that was almost unbearable.

Alex gazed at her, all expression draining from his face. His eyes had a curiously shuttered look.

'So, I was able to take your mind off your fear for a few minutes,' he said coolly. 'How nice to be of service.'

Elyn ran unsteady fingers through her damp curls, then tucked her shirt into the waistband of her trousers, not daring to meet his ironic stare.

'Ye—yes,' she stuttered, 'but, of course, I shall make quite sure it doesn't happen again.'

Something blazed briefly in Alex's eyes, but his voice was the sardonic drawl she knew and hated.

'Were my kisses so distasteful? I could have sworn you were enjoying them. But I've heard that the talent to pretend is something women acquire with experience.'

His words cut like a whiplash. Elyn looked down at her tightly-clasped hands. What could she say? He had been making insinuations about her past ever since her arrival. But if she denied them, if she told him that no-one had ever stirred her as he had, that where he was concerned she was incapable of pretence, he could hardly fail to realise the truth of her feelings for him. He was a highly astute man, and had already shown a disconcerting ability to read her thoughts. If she revealed, by the smallest slip, that she was in love with him, he would dismiss her on the spot, and despite the enormous problems this shattering realisation was going to cause her, Elyn wanted to keep the job to which she was becoming more committed as each busy day passed.

She bit her lip. She must remain silent. Let him think what he would.

Alex's glance hardened into something approaching contempt. He turned away from her, his jaw set, and opened his door. The wind had dropped as suddenly as it had risen and the gloom was lightening every second as the dust and sand settled.

'Where are you going?' Elyn blurted.

'To clear the sand from the wheels so we can get away from here,' he rasped.

'Do you want some help? Shall I—?'

His reply was so brusque that Elyn flinched. 'Stay where you are.' He slammed the door with such force the vehicle rocked.

Within minutes he was back. He climbed in and started the engine, and, carefully easing the Land Rover free of the soft sand, he swung it onto the track. Though covered by a fresh layer of dust and sand, it was marked by stones at each side.

The rest of the drive back was a nightmare for Elyn, as she tried to come to terms with her love for Alex, and the knowledge that from now on her job was going to be an exquisite agony. Working with him every day and having to be constantly on her guard against letting slip even the slightest hint of the love she felt for him was going to be the hardest task she had ever undertaken. Yet she felt privileged to work with him, and if a bruised heart and iron self-control were the price she had to pay, then she'd do it gladly.

A painful smile touched her lips when she recalled how she had struggled to disguise her dislike of him. She had really believed she hated him. How strange was the human heart. The forces of love and hate were so very close, two sides of the same coin. How devastating was their confusion!

Alex too was silent, giving all his attention to driving, pushing the Land Rover to its limits, as if anxious to reach Khalifa as quickly as possible. It occurred to Elyn to wonder why, as the sandstorm was now past. Of course, there was the unpacking to do, and evening rounds. But Elyn suspected that his over-riding desire was to be rid of her company.

They roared into the compound. Alex braked the Land Rover to a halt in front of the clinic and was out, slamming the door, almost before it had stopped.

Elyn climbed out more slowly, stiff from the bumpy ride, and sticky from the dust and heat. She felt grubby, dishevelled and emotionally exhausted and longed for a shower.

As she walked round to join Alex who had just unlocked the rear door of the Land Rover, the glass doors of the clinic opened and Samina, cool and elegant in a skirt and jacket of turquoise linen, stood poised on the verandah. Her raven hair was gathered into an immaculate chignon, and her make-up, even in the late afternoon heat, was flawless.

Her brows arched in surprise and her eyes narrowed fractionally as she caught sight of Elyn. Then, she walked lightly down the steps and, passing Elyn as though she didn't exist, Samina drifted up to Alex and, slipping both arms around him, kissed him full on the mouth.

'Hello, darling,' she throbbed in her husky voice, 'I thought I'd surprise you.'

'You certainly did that,' Alex said drily as he gently pulled her arms from his neck. 'Why don't you wait inside where it's cooler and I'll be with you in a moment when I've finished unloading.'

'Please,' Elyn said quickly to Alex, surprised she was able to speak at all so great was her shock at the Egyptian's unexpected appearance, 'I'll deal with the unloading.' She didn't even glance at Samina who had one arm hooked through Alex's, as if proclaiming ownership. 'You must entertain your—friend.'

Alex flashed her a quizzical glance, but Elyn moved swiftly to pull out the first of the boxes.

'Of course, you're right,' Alex agreed, all too quickly. It seemed to Elyn he could hardly wait to be alone with Samina, yet the taste of his kisses was still fresh on her lips.

'I'll send Mohammed out to unload the general supplies. You just handle the drugs and stuff for the pharmacy.'

Elyn nodded, almost snatching the lists from him. She began lifting out the boxes, placing them in two piles, willing Alex to go and take Samina with him. She sensed the other woman's derisive gaze and anger bubbled inside her. Fate seemed to be making cruel sport of her emotions.

Why was it that on both the occasions she had encountered Samina, the elegant Egyptian looked cool and beautiful and totally in command of the situation, while she was hot, dishevelled and barely in control of anything. Elyn knew that in Samina's eyes she was an object of derision.

As if in confirmation Samina, leaving a trace of her musky perfume on the still, afternoon air, gazed up at Alex as they turned away and without bothering to lower her voice asked, 'Isn't that the silly girl who made such trouble with her luggage at the airport? What is she doing out here, Alex? Don't tell me you have given her a job? Surely there's enough cheap labour in the oasis—?'

'Come along inside, Samina,' Alex cut in smoothly, 'no doubt you'd like some tea. Then perhaps you'll tell me what brings you out here today.'

Their voices faded as they entered the clinic and the doors swung shut. Elyn bit her lip hard, and swallowed the stiffness in her throat. He had not uttered one word in her defence, he hadn't offered *her* any tea, though after the traumatic experiences of the afternoon she longed for a cup of the soothing, refreshing brew.

Another fit of anger shook Elyn. Cheap labour? Who did that spoilt, perfectly groomed, immaculate clothes horse think she was?

Elyn rubbed the back of her hand across her forehead, feeling its stickiness as she freed the damp curls that clung to her skin. She glanced down at her damp and dusty shirt and trousers and her normal common sense and good humour asserted themselves in a giggle that took her by surprise. She certainly did look like cheap labour.

Elyn shook her head, sighed and gave a mental shrug. Let them both think what they like. She must get on with her work, and put Alex and Samina out of her mind. If she just concentrated on the job in hand, ignoring everything else, she would cope beautifully.

Elyn was tempted to dawdle in the pharmacy, taking longer than strictly necessary to put away the drugs. But her sense of duty to the patients and a strong desire to get the working day finished so that she could escape to the privacy of her bungalow, urged her on.

She locked the pharmacy door and hurried down the corridor to Alex's office to file the lists.

Pushing open the door, her eyes on the sheaf of papers in her hand, she was brought to a sudden halt by the sight of Samina resting one shapely hip on Alex's desk as she leaned across it to murmur in his ear, revealing a long expanse of tanned leg.

'Please excuse me,' Elyn said crisply, recovering almost at once, 'the drug lists—'

'Thank you, Dr Scott,' Alex met her eyes coolly, and Elyn felt a pang at his formality. 'Just file them, will you?'

Samina straightened up, her movements fluid and graceful, a smile playing at the corners of her full mouth. 'Alex tells me you're actually a doctor,' she purred throatily as Elyn bent to the filing cabinet. 'I'm afraid I thought you were just a—what is the word—skivvy.' Her insincere smile widened in self-deprecation, but her eyes remained cold.

Elyn glanced at her as she placed the lists in the folder. 'A natural mistake under the circumstances,' she said lightly and slammed the cabinet drawer closed. Just then Jehan entered the office from the ward.

'Doesn't anyone ever knock before coming into your office, Alex?' Samina pouted in complaint. 'In Daddy's clinic nursing staff and junior doctors show more respect—'

Alex ignored her. 'Yes, Jehan?'

The senior nurse's face was carefully blank. 'I was wondering if you intended to do ward rounds before or after evening meal, Doctor.' She turned to Elyn. 'You wish for tea, Dr Scott?'

Elyn was about to accept the welcome invitation when Samina cut in.

'We've had ours,' she said languidly, studying her nails, 'besides, Nurse, you did say you were busy.'

'Then I won't trouble you, Jehan,' Elyn shook her head ruefully, 'you've obviously got enough to do.'

Jehan's face remained impassive, but her eyes could not mask her dislike as she glared briefly at Samina before giving Elyn a small, warm smile. 'For you, *hanem*, is no trouble.'

Elyn felt ridiculously pleased. At least she had one ally in this difficult place. Then guilt pricked her. This was no way to behave. She was here to care for sick people, not worry about scoring points off some gorgeous visitor who wasn't important.

But she was important, a small voice inside Elyn nagged. She and Alex were obviously very close. They had obviously been friends for quite a while, judging by Samina's casual way of dropping in unannounced and unexpected, and equally obviously their friendship was not purely platonic.

Elyn's fingers clenched involuntarily as a shaft of pure jealousy knifed through her. She controlled herself instantly, forcing her mind back to the business in hand.

'Jehan, you're an angel, but I'll wait till I finish. We've both got work to do.' She turned to Alex, suddenly reckless.

'Shall I do rounds this evening, Dr Davidson? You seem to have your hands full.'

Anger blazed in the depths of Alex's green eyes, but was gone in an instant, leaving Elyn to wonder if she had imagined it.

His reply was a sardonic drawl. 'Thank you, Dr Scott. It has been a somewhat tedious day. I shall enjoy the opportunity to relax in such desirable company.' The smile he turned on Samina changed his whole face, lighting his normally forbidding countenance with a warmth Elyn had never seen before. Samina almost purred.

Feeling the knife twist in her heart, Elyn turned to Jehan. 'Shall we go?' she said briskly, and with head held high, she edged past Alex's desk out into the ward, with Jehan close behind.

'That woman,' Jehan hissed as soon as the office door was closed, 'she is trouble, she and her father—' Jehan broke into a torrent of Arabic, which, judging from the expression on her plump face, was anything but complimentary. 'She try to make Dr Davidson leave clinic here, go work for her father at his private clinic in Cairo.'

Elyn swung round on Jehan, torn between wanting to know more, and obeying the rules of professional etiquette which forbade one doctor discussing another with nursing staff. Elyn was surprised at Jehan, who was usually a model of correct behaviour, and demanded the same standards from her nurses. Samina had obviously upset her deeply.

'I'm sure Dr Davidson will not be persuaded to do anything against his will.' Elyn spoke more sharply than she intended, in an effort to quell her own doubts.

What if Alex were to leave Khalifa? What would become of this clinic? Elyn had been here only a short time, but already she felt part of it, deeply involved and concerned with the people it served. No-one else would devote the amount of time and energy to the work here that Alex did. What would happen to the people of the oasis, and the proud Bedouin, whose trust and respect Alex had worked for months to gain.

Putting aside the fact that she loved him, Elyn was clear-eyed enough to realise that a doctor with Alex's talents in medicine, surgery and administration was a rarity. And while she realised it was vital that he remain here, the question nagged, what had brought him here in the first place?

'As you say, *hanem*,' Jehan's face immediately assumed an expression of polite acquiescence, effectively putting a cool distance between Elyn and herself.

Elyn was about to apologise, to explain that the

information had surprised and worried her, when she was engulfed by a wave of impatience and indignation. It seemed that everyone was tearing little bits off her. She was being dragged in all directions at once. She had had enough. She just wanted to get the day over with and escape from them all to her own little bungalow.

'I'll rinse my face and hands, Jehan, then we'll begin with Hamid,' Elyn said, matching Jehan's coolness with her own.

When she had completed the rounds, writing up the notes as she went and checking the evening drug doses, she asked Jehan to return the files to Alex's office, unwilling to face the possibility of encountering Alex and Samina again that day. She was too tired and too emotionally exhausted to be sure of her ability to remain calm and outwardly untouched by the sight of them together.

Leaving Jehan to hand over to Magda and the night staff, Elyn slipped out of the back door. She shivered as the chill of the desert evening struck her. As she walked across the compound she looked up at the black velvet sky where brilliant stars, like handfuls of carelessly flung diamonds, sparkled coldly.

Elyn breathed in deeply. The air rushed into her lungs like chilled wine, cleansing, revitalising, sweeping away the staleness and tension of the day. As she drew near Alex's house, she glanced up involuntarily, then wished with all her heart she had kept her eyes averted.

There, in the centre of the sitting room with the lamps bathing them in golden light, stood Alex and Samina, swaying, wrapped in each other's arms, their mouths locked in a kiss.

The impact of the scene was like a kick in the stomach to Elyn. She gasped at the pain and her hand flew to her own lips as she froze, unable to move, unable to tear her eyes away.

Samina had changed out of her turquoise outfit and was now wearing a filmy gown of midnight blue. Her raven hair tumbled loosely over her bare shoulders and her golden skin gleamed like satin in the soft glow of the oil lamps.

Alex had also changed. The cream short-sleeved shirt and pale slacks emphasised his dark good looks.

Suddenly, as if aware of the watcher, Alex detached himself from the entwining arms and came to the window. He stood unmoving, looking out into the darkness.

Elyn wanted to run, to hide, but her feet refused to obey. She was rooted to the spot. Then, after what seemed like ages, but was in fact only one or two seconds, he opened wide his arms, and in one abrupt, sweeping movement, drew the curtains together, shutting out the night, and Elyn.

The spell was broken. Her heart thudding as if she had run for miles, Elyn stumbled across to her own bungalow and, slamming the door, leaned against it while she fought to regain her self-control.

If this was love, this aching hurt, this gnawing jealousy, this hopelessness, then she wanted none of it.

Wearily, Elyn walked into the kitchen. Nefra had gone, leaving a cold meal prepared on a tray. Elyn was thankful that she need keep up the pretence no longer.

Stepping into the shower, she turned on the taps. As the warm water washed the dust and sweat from her body, she let the tears come.

Sometime later, Elyn was roused from restless, troubled dreams by the sound of a small aircraft. It barely penetrated her consciousness, but as the engine noise faded, Elyn turned over, found a cool place on the pillow and slipped into a deep, dreamless sleep.

At eleven the following morning, Jehan literally dragged Elyn from the Outpatient's Department, pushed her into the office, which was fortunately empty, and sat her down in Alex's chair.

'You don't move, *hanem*,' she said severely, 'I bring coffee.'

Elyn made to get up. 'Jehan, I don't have time. When I've finished the Trachoma Clinic, Dr Davidson will need me to help with the bilharzia cases.'

'So, you need coffee now,' Jehan stated firmly. '*Hanem*, you no good doctor if too tired, make mistake.'

Elyn's head snapped up, her mouth opened to protest, then, realising the truth of the Chief Nurse's statement she nodded, and leaned back in the chair, lifting her aching feet onto the desk. She sighed with relief at being off her legs for a moment.

This was the first time she had sat down, or even paused for breath since 7.30 that morning, when an influx of patients had begun. Brought on ox-carts, on donkey litters or even carried, the trickle had become a flood and Alex had set up a triage on the verandah to determine who should be admitted and who must, after outpatients treatment, be returned home.

The nurses and paramedics darted about even more swiftly than usual.

Elyn had approached the clinic in some trepidation that morning. The latter half of the night she had slept well and she had woken refreshed and strangely calm. Her acknowledgement to herself of her love for Alex had marked a significant change in her attitude to being at the clinic. Her constant feeling of tension, of aggression towards him, had disappeared, leaving in its wake a fatalistic acceptance of the fact that though she loved him, he could never love her. She quickly suppressed the aching void that opened up before her as a picture of life after her contract expired and she had left the clinic, flashed into her mind. She could not, must not think about that. She must strive for normality, for total professionalism. That was what she was here for. All else must be ignored.

As it happened, her task was made easier by the scenes of frantic activity which met her the instant she stepped inside the door.

The first person she saw was Alex. Her heart thumped unevenly at the sight of his lean, lithe figure striding swiftly across the passage ahead of her. He halted as he caught sight of her.

She waited nervously for his first words. Would he make any reference to the traumatic happenings of yesterday? But of course for him they had not been traumatic. His reactions had revealed nothing more than irritation and amusement. Anyway, surely the appearance of Samina Youssef had erased from his mind the episode in the Land Rover, which for Elyn had been a turning point in her life.

She need not have worried, his mind was totally occupied with medical matters, which, Elyn decided later, must have explained the warmth of his greeting.

'Glad you're here,' Alex said quickly, a brief smile cracking the grim expression on his face, lightening his eyes in a way that flooded Elyn with melting heat and turned her knees to water.

She felt her colour rise but resolutely ignored it, berating herself for her startled reaction and said in her most businesslike manner, 'What's the trouble?' Then, before he could answer, she remembered. 'The canal? Bilharzia?'

He nodded, his face set. 'They started coming in during the night and things are getting really hectic now.'

'Is it acute?'

'Yes, high fever, headache, and allergic skin reactions that will probably last several weeks. Thank God we got the new drug supplies yesterday.' He appeared not to notice Elyn's cheeks suddenly flame.

'What do you want me to do?' Elyn asked, noticing as she looked up at him the lines of weariness and tension at the corners of his eyes and mouth. How she longed to smooth them away with gentle fingers. She caught herself. The best way to help was not to dream impossible dreams, but to do her job and shoulder her share of the burden.

'I was just on my way to the pharmacy, but it would be more useful if you prepared the injections. The initial adult dose is 1ml of 6% solution of antimony lithium thiomalate.'

'How many?'

'Prepare thirty, to begin with.'

'We don't have enough disposable syringes, so I'll get one of the trainees to stay with the steriliser.' Elyn was thinking swiftly. 'What about emetine or antimony sodium tartrate, shall I make up those, too?'

He thought deeply for a few seconds.

'Not for the moment. They have to be administered intravenously and are highly toxic, which means nursing at rest, and we simply don't have the facilities. Let's start with the lithium. If we increase it until four times the amount can be tolerated on alternate days, up to a total of 40–60 ml, it should be sufficient to eliminate the parasite from the body. After that—' he shrugged.

Elyn knew what he meant, only the patients themselves could decide whether or not to risk re-infection in the affected water.

'I'll do it straight away,' Elyn began to move past him.

'After that, will you do ward rounds for our usual patients and then you'll have to manage the trachoma clinic. I'll look in if I have the chance.'

Elyn opened her mouth but he was gone, striding down the corridor. She closed it. What was there to say? She wanted to share the load, well here was her chance. Taking a deep breath, she hurried into the pharmacy.

Slumped in Alex's chair, Elyn sipped the strong, steaming coffee Jehan had brought her before rushing back to the mêlée on her wards. She closed her eyes and leaned her head back against the wall behind her, deliberately shutting off all thought, letting her body relax completely.

The office door opened and, assuming it was Jehan, Elyn, not bothering to open her eyes, murmured as she swallowed the last of her coffee, 'You've just saved my life.'

'I'm glad to hear it,' the deep sardonic tones of Alex's voice made her start violently. Her eyes flew open and as she leapt to her feet, she crashed the cup down onto the saucer so hard, chips flew off. Elyn's face was crimson.

'I was just—I mean—'

'So I see,' Alex retorted drily. 'Well, if you've quite finished, perhaps you'd get back to those sick children? That is, of course, if you've nothing more important to do?' His cool sarcasm pierced Elyn like a blade. A torrent of angry words rose to her lips, but she bit them back. She would not make excuses or grovel.

Head high and eyes bright with suppressed anger, Elyn moved round the desk, but he barred her way.

He towered over her, his hands on his hips, his whites providing startling contrast to his tanned skin and rumpled black hair.

'Kindly let me pass,' Elyn felt her heart give a sudden lurch as she stopped in front of him. He didn't move. He just stood, staring down at her, his face implacable, a strange light in his eyes. Elyn wanted to step back, to move away from him. He was too close, she felt drawn towards him as if by a magnet. She would have to move back. But that would mean admitting defeat in this silent battle waging between them. Elyn felt the tension rising. She couldn't take much more.

'Get out of the way,' her voice rose, and in sheer exasperation she lifted her hands to his chest to push him back.

In an instant his arms were around her, two steel bands crushing her against him, making her all too aware of the hardness of his masculine body.

'Let me go,' Elyn gasped, unable to move.

He looked down at her, his green eyes as cold and stormy as winter seas. 'Nobody talks to me like that,' he said softly, sending a thrill of terror through Elyn. 'Nobody,' he repeated. Then, without warning, he brought his head down and fastened his mouth on hers, his kiss cruel and punishing, bruising her lips. Inside Elyn a soft explosion sent dark flames shooting through her, her toes and fingers tingled and her head spun.

Just as Elyn thought she was about to faint for lack of air, he released her, stepping back so suddenly she staggered and would have fallen down had she not bumped against the desk. She clung to it for support.

'Perhaps you'll remember in future,' he said, seeming untouched by the incident, but his eyes as he gazed down at her held a curious expression, of mingled shock and self-contempt.

'You beast,' Elyn whispered, wiping a trembling hand across her mouth as if to scrub away all memory of contact with him. 'How—how could you?' She broke off, her head bowed like a broken flower, fighting the tears that suddenly threatened to overwhelm her. He might not like her, but to degrade her with that travesty of a kiss, a vicious mockery of a contact which should signify at least affection and respect, if not passionate love, that was unforgiveable.

He stared at her a moment longer, his face unreadable, then, turning away, he strode out of the office and down the corridor.

Elyn tried to steady her ragged breathing. She had to get back to the Outpatients Clinic. A vivid picture of the children who were waiting, their crusted, swollen eyelids evidence of the conjunctivitis which caused scarring of the eyeball, leading to blindness, helped her pull herself together.

Though Alex hadn't known it, she'd had no chance to tell him, her short coffee break had given Elyn's nurse assistant time to unpack and prepare more sterile dressings, also to sterilise another batch of syringes necessary to administer the injections of sulphonamides and tetracyclines with which they were fighting the disease.

Elyn threw herself into her work, committing herself totally to the patients, leaving no space or time for personal thoughts of any kind. Lunch was a hasty snack swallowed while she made notes on the cards which made up the outpatient filing system.

It was three-thirty and she had only one more patient

to see, a toffee-coloured little boy whose milky pupils showed all too clearly the damage caused by the chlamydia organism.

Making a mental note to ask Alex about the possibility of cornea transplants, Elyn gave the boy his injection and was washing her hands while the nurse tidied up, when the sound of a Land Rover entering the compound caught her attention.

She was wondering who it could be, when the door flew open and Tim Preston, his sandy hair all awry, and a wide grin splitting his freckled face, burst in.

'Surprise!' he said, opening his arms wide and dropping on one knee in the time-honoured manner of one expecting applause.

After her initial shock, Elyn burst out laughing and her spirits rose instantly.

'Tim! I didn't expect to see you. What are you doing out here?'

Tim clambered to his feet and shrugged elaborately. 'Where else could I find a woman with grace, beauty, intelligence and a wonderful bedside manner, which I'm longing to try out?' He seized her hand and kissed it rapidly several times.

'Oh, you idiot,' Elyn laughed. Something niggled at her, Tim was almost too bright, too effusive. But it was so good to see a friendly face, so nice to be flattered and paid court to, however insincere, she pushed the warning voice aside, determined to ignore it. Her emotions had been battered enough lately, she was heartsore and weary. How soothing to have Tim pouring silly nonsense over her like warm honey.

'I refuse to believe that's the only reason you've come. After all, you didn't know whether I'd be free. In fact I'm not. We've got a panic on at the moment, a bilharzia outbreak.'

Tim nodded sympathetically, his grin fading. 'Actually, you're right. There is another reason, though I'm sorry to have to add to your troubles.'

'What is it? What's the matter?' Elyn glanced up from

the card drawer, lifting it back into the filing cabinet.
One of the runners stuck.

'Here, let me,' Tim stepped forward and freed it and
the drawer slid smoothly closed. 'I'm afraid it's Henry
Barnes. Maud radioed through to the hospital at Kharga
this morning, and they tried to phone you, but the line's
out again. So I said I'd bring the message. Anyway it
gave me the chance to see my favourite doctor again.'

'What message,' Elyn frowned. 'What's wrong with
Henry?'

'Malaria,' Tim replied, 'or rather a relapse. Seems he
ran out of Paludrine.'

'Where is he?'

'A few miles to the north-east. They were on their way
here to get more anti-malaria pills when Henry was
taken ill.'

'Do you know how bad he is?' Elyn felt real concern.
Relapses were quite common in people who had had
malaria, but varied in severity depending on the type of
parasite carried by the mosquito.

Tim grimaced. 'Maud was pretty worried, said he had
high fever and was babbling and he had the shakes.'

'We've got to get him in right away. Nurse.' Elyn
caught the girl as she hurried through with a tray of
syringes for the steriliser, 'where is Mohammed and the
ambulance?'

'He take patients to homes, *hanem*, and bring more,'
the girl replied haltingly.

'Well, that's out,' Elyn bit her lip, then made a sudden
decision.

'Look Tim, I know it's a bit much to ask, but would
you take me to pick up Henry. Alex—Dr Davidson,'
she hastily corrected herself, 'can't go, and the ambulance is busy. I've just finished here and we should
be back before I have to do ward rounds. Would you
mind?'

Tim grinned, 'For you, anything. Glad to be of service. I always wanted to do a heroic rescue.'

'Thanks, Tim, I do appreciate it, so will Maud. I've

just got to collect what I need from the pharmacy and I'll be with you.'

Tim stepped forward. 'Why don't I come with you,' he said quickly. 'It'll only take half the time.'

'No,' Elyn shook her head, memories of Alex's warnings against Tim all too clear. If Alex should catch sight of him now heaven only knew what conclusions he'd jump to, regardless of the fact that Tim was here for a legitimate reason. 'It won't take long. You wait in the Land Rover.'

'Go on, Elyn. I can help, I'm really quite useful, let me give you a hand,' he pressed and Elyn sensed an undercurrent that disturbed her. But there was no time to consider it further.

'Thanks all the same, Tim,' she said decisively, 'but it really would be better if you waited outside.'

He shrugged crossly. 'All right, all right, I'm going.' He looked over his shoulder and an apologetic grin lifted one corner of his mouth.

'Sorry,' he said. 'It's just that I've got a swine of a headache. Couldn't let me have something for it, could you?'

Elyn, her mind already busy on the task ahead, nodded absently, 'Of course, I'll bring you a couple of codeine. The nurse will get you some water.'

'Thanks,' Tim gave a shaky laugh, 'er—you haven't got anything stronger, have you? Codeine doesn't seem to work too well for me.'

Elyn shot him a glance, then, anxious to get started, she nodded quickly. 'I'll have a look. You wait here.'

They bumped and rattled up the trail out of the oasis onto the plateau. Elyn looked surreptitiously at Tim as he wrestled with the Land Rover. Something about him worried her, but she couldn't put her finger on it.

'Your headache easing?' she asked.

He nodded. 'Yes thanks, whatever you gave me certainly did the trick. You're a real angel of mercy. My little desert flower.'

'And you're all blarney,' Elyn retorted smiling. 'Just

the same, it might be an idea for you to get a check-up at
Kharga Hospital or here at the clinic. I'm sure Dr
Davidson would have a look at you if you can wait
until the bilharzia epidemic eases off.'

'No,' Tim said so sharply, Elyn stared at him. He
immediately tried to laugh off his abruptness. 'No, I'm
fine, I'd just be wasting his time and it seems that he's
kept quite busy enough without wasting his precious
time on a simple migraine.'

Elyn shrugged, not wanting to press the point, Tim
was right, Alex did have more than enough to do.
Besides, although the tablets she had given Tim were
more powerful than a simple headache remedy, they did
seem to have done the trick. Tim was much more relaxed
now, his brittleness seemed to have worn off and he'd
stopped scratching his nose in that nervy manner.

What other alternative had there been? Elyn asked
herself. It was imperative she reached Henry as soon as
possible and with no-one else to take her, she hadn't
really had any choice.

But the niggle remained, the feeling she had overlooked something, something important.

CHAPTER SIX

'How much further?' Elyn asked worriedly, as they
roared across the plateau, their dust trail fogging the
shimmering air.

'Shouldn't be long now,' Tim replied, his sandy brows
knitted in concentration while sweat beaded his face. He
glanced at the compass mounted above the dashboard.
'Keep your eyes peeled, we're on the right heading.
Thank heaven Maud had the sense to give us a compass
bearing.'

Elyn peered ahead through the windscreen, anxiously
searching the flat, desolate terrain for any sign of life.
But the heat reflected off the barren, stony surface
caused the ground to waver, as though beneath moving
water. Elyn blinked hard a few times, then she grabbed
Tim's arm.

'There, over there,' she pointed. 'That khaki splodge,
by the low hill, isn't that a vehicle? I think I see a tent
beside it.'

Tim followed her pointing finger. 'That's them,' he
confirmed, and swung the Land Rover towards the small
rectangle of canvas, partially shaded by the Barnes's
battered Land Rover.

As they drew closer a figure stumbled through the
flaps of the tent. It was Maud, wearing lime-green
trousers and an orange shirt. She staggered a little as she
stood upright, pressing one hand to her back while she
waved wildly with the other.

'She needn't have bothered to wave,' Tim remarked
sourly, 'we could hardly have missed her in that outfit.'
He braked the Land Rover to a skidding halt and flicked
off the engine. The silence was suddenly loud.

Elyn grabbed her medical bag and leapt out, running
towards the tent. Maud came forward to greet her.

'Oh, my dear, I'm so glad to see you. I've been that worried—couldn't Alex come? I suppose he's busy as usual—'

Elyn opened her mouth to explain about the bilharzia epidemic, but Maud gave her no chance.

'It's Henry—malaria—it was so sudden—and I'm afraid—' her plump, good-natured face suddenly crumpled and she quickly turned her head away.

Elyn put an arm round her shoulders. 'It's all right, Maud. We'll get him back to the clinic as soon as I've had a look at him.' She gave the older woman a quick squeeze. 'Go and ask Tim for the vacuum jug, I put some ice in it just before we left.'

Giving Maud a gentle push, Elyn turned and bent down to enter the tent. Though Maud had tied back the flaps at both ends to catch the faintest breath of air, the atmosphere inside the tent was stuffy and foetid.

Kneeling beside the folding canvas bed, Elyn noted the hectic flush of fever and the deep lines of exhaustion that had aged Henry ten years in the few weeks since she had last seen him.

As Elyn checked his pulse and opened her bag, taking out the sphygmomanometer and wrapping the thin canvas cuff around Henry's upper arm, Maud crawled back into the tent with the vacuum jug.

Elyn glanced up as she pumped the rubber ball to inflate the cuff. 'Wrap a handful of ice-cubes in each of two towels, to make a couple of ice-packs, Maud, then soak as many towels as you can in whatever ice-water is left.'

Maud nodded, her small bright eyes darting anxiously from her husband to Elyn and back again as Elyn continued her examination.

'He's got a high fever and his spleen is definitely enlarged,' she told Maud. 'When did he have his last paludrine tablet?'

Maud screwed up her perspiring face with the effort of remembering. 'It must have been two, no three days ago. He mislaid the bottle. We were going to come and see you and get some more before going on to Kharga. I mean, I didn't think there was any panic—but then—then—' she broke off, her lips trembling and her normally cheerful face stricken as she relived her husband's sudden collapse.

'Have you got those packs ready?' Elyn pressed gently. 'I want to try and get his temperature down as quickly as possible, his heart is under enough strain as it is.'

Suddenly Henry moaned and flung his arm up. His hand, on which he wore a scarab ring, hit Elyn high on her cheek, knocking her sideways. Maud gasped, but Elyn reassured her with a quick smile and she seized Henry's arm as rigors shook him and he began to mutter incoherently.

Wiping the inside of his elbow with a swab soaked in spirit, Elyn turned to Maud. 'Hold his arm steady,' she directed as she prepared the hypodermic, breaking the top from a glass phial and drawing the clear fluid into the syringe.

'This is camoquin,' she explained to Maud who was watching wide-eyed, clinging to her husband's arm in an effort to keep it still while violent tremors shuddered through him. 'It will reduce the symptoms and enable us to get him back to the clinic for proper rest and nursing.'

She administered the injection quickly and repacked the syringe and used phial in their small padded box. 'Hang on there a minute, Maud, I'll get Tim to help us.'

Soon they had Henry laid on his canvas bed in the back of Tim's Land Rover, surrounded by cool wet towels with one ice pack on his forehead and another over his chest. Elyn scrambled out of the vehicle, leaving Maud to watch over her husband who already seemed to be resting more peacefully.

Tim had finished dismantling the tent. 'I've thrown all the rest of their gear into their own vehicle. Once this is folded, we're ready to go. Which do you want me to drive?'

Elyn thought for a moment. 'You know the route and

you know the ground better than I do. You'd better drive your own vehicle with Maud and Henry in it, and I'll follow in theirs. If Maud has any problems she can signal me and I'll sound my horn. Drive as fast but as smoothly as you can.'

'You're the doctor,' Tim grinned and Elyn noticed a sickly pallor beneath his freckles.

As if aware of her scrutiny, Tim flung the rolled canvas into the back, slammed the door and hurried forward to his own vehicle. 'Let's go, Doc,' he sang over his shoulder.

By the time they arrived back at the clinic, Elyn's arms and shoulders were stiff and aching with the effort of holding the heavy Land Rover on course, while keeping one eye on the vehicle in front in case Maud signalled.

The two vehicles stopped outside the verandah and Elyn climbed out and opened the back of Tim's to help Maud.

'We'll carry him in on the bed, it will be quicker,' she decided. 'Just a moment, I'll get Tim to give us a hand.' She hurried to the front and pulled the door open. Tim looked up, startled.

'What on earth are you doing?' Elyn demanded as she saw her medical bag open beside him, its contents scattered over the worn leather seat and the floor.

Tim recovered instantly and started replacing the boxes, tins and phials. 'It slid off when I stopped, and landed upside down. The catch must be loose, for when I went to pick it up, the whole lot just fell out. I think I've found everything.' He snapped the bag shut and fiddled with the catch.

'You ought to get that seen to, Elyn. You could lose something important. You carry dangerous drugs in there, don't you?'

Elyn eyed him uncertainly. 'Yes—some, but only in small quantities.' She reached for the bag and he pushed it towards her. 'But you're right. I'll get the catch checked. Now, could you give us a hand to get Henry into the clinic. The paramedics aren't back yet and I want him under observation on the ward as soon as possible.'

'Being a bit over-cautious, aren't you?' Tim needled. 'Still trying to impress the boss?'

Elyn turned aside so he would not see the rush of colour to her face. 'I told you once before, Tim, I wouldn't waste my time,' she tossed the words over her shoulder. 'Alex Davidson is not easily impressed.' That's the understatement of the century, she thought to herself. 'And I'm not being over-cautious,' she went on. 'A malarial relapse at Henry's age on top of a heart condition could very easily prove fatal,' she retorted sharply. 'Now will you help or shall I send for a trainee nurse?'

Tim clambered out. 'Simmer down, lady. I'm now put firmly in my place,' He grinned lopsidedly, 'Course I'll help.'

After they reached the ward Tim waited by the nurses' cubicle while Maud helped one of the trainees put Henry to bed. Jehan cornered Elyn to request medication for Ali, the patient with the arm injury.

'Dr Davidson too busy in Female Ward, I no disturb him. But Ali got severe pain, *hanem*, can't rest, his temperature going higher.'

Elyn frowned. 'He can't have any more morphine. We'd better give him Omnopon. It has almost the same pain-relief and sedative effects, but without the risks. Better make it one-third of a grain.' She handed Jehan her keys. 'Will you bring the powder from the pharmacy while I check Mr Barnes?'

The Chief Nurse nodded and hurried away.

Elyn gave Henry a quick but thorough examination. The ride through the desert did not appear to have made his condition any worse, but he looked exhausted and frail, which worried Maud. While Elyn was calming her, Jehan returned.

'I put the Omnopon in nurses' cubicle, *hanem*. My pupil is fetching sterile syringe and distilled water from the steriliser on Female Ward. All ours using up on bilharzia cases,' and she rushed away down the crowded ward, before Elyn, who had missed her first words, could ask her to repeat them.

A light touch on Elyn's shoulder turned her round. Tim was standing behind her. Maud excused herself and returned to Henry's side.

It seemed to Elyn that Tim looked anxious and edgy. He was moving from one foot to the other and continually glancing round him. But Elyn didn't take too much notice. Hospitals affected a lot of people that way, making them nervous and uneasy.

'I'd better be on my way,' he said quickly. 'I've done all I can, and I'm just in the way now.'

'You've been an enormous help,' Elyn smiled warmly at him. 'Honestly, I don't know how we'd have managed without you.'

He looked even more uncomfortable. 'OK, OK, it was no big deal. Look, I must go. I'll be seeing you, Elyn, soon as I can. We must get together, without the audience—' suddenly his eyes widened, and his expression froze and he almost ran from the ward.

Elyn stared after him for a moment, then turned to see what had precipitated his abrupt departure.

Down the ward with a face like thunder strode Alex Davidson. 'Was that Preston I saw scuttling out?' he demanded, tightly controlling his obvious fury.

'Yes, but it wasn't a social call,' Elyn replied hastily. 'He brought a message from Kharga as our phone line is out again. Maud Barnes had radioed for help. Henry had had a recurrence of malaria—'

'What was Preston doing on the ward?' Alex rapped.

'I'm trying to explain,' Elyn snapped back, her eyes flashing. His arrogance was positively infuriating. She pressed her nails into her palms in an effort to contain her quick anger.

Amusement lit his eyes for an instant, though his expression remained forbidding. 'Then please don't let me stop you,' came the dry rejoinder and his dark brow lifted in silent query as he waited for her explanation.

Elyn had an overwhelming urge to hit him, to pound his broad chest with her fists, to shatter his rock-like composure. But also, beneath her frustrated anger ran a deeper current, a longing to touch him, to feel again the warmth and movement of his muscular body beneath her hands.

Shocked by her own treacherous thoughts, Elyn swallowed convulsively, moistening her dry lips with the tip of her tongue.

'There was no-one in the clinic free to help me and Henry needed constant watching during the journey, which meant Maud staying beside him. If I'd gone alone, even supposing I'd been able to find them, it would have meant them leaving their Land Rover and all their belongings out in the desert. So I asked Tim to drive me,' she finished defiantly.

Alex nodded briefly. 'Has Preston been left alone in the clinic at all? Think, Elyn, it's important.'

Elyn frowned and racked her brain, trying to remember. It had been such a hectic day, with so much going on, recalling details was not easy. 'I don't think so. He offered to help me in the pharmacy,' she recalled, then seeing the look on Alex's face, added quickly, 'but I asked him to wait in the Land Rover. You two don't seem exactly friendly,' She probed tentatively, hoping Alex would volunteer the reason behind the antipathy between himself and Tim. But he ignored her remark.

'And you noticed nothing odd? His behaviour was quite normal?' Alex pressed.

'I don't know what you're getting at,' Elyn shrugged helplessly. 'Tim couldn't have been more helpful, especially as he had a bad headache when he arrived.'

'Did he indeed,' Alex frowned. 'Did he ask you for anything?'

'Not specifically, but I gave him a couple of Methadone tablets as he said codeine didn't agree with him. After that he seemed better, though I do think his nerves aren't too good, he seems a bit twitchy. Like the rest of us, he's probably working too hard. Oh,' a thought occurred to Elyn, 'is there someone who could look at the clasp on my medical bag?'

'Why? What's the matter with it?' Alex frowned.

'Tim said it shot off the seat when he stopped the Land Rover and everything fell out.' Elyn shook her head. 'It's funny though, I hadn't noticed anything wrong with it.'

'Let me get this straight,' Alex's face darkened, 'Tim had your medical bag? Do you leave it lying about for anyone to help themselves? For crying out loud, Elyn, where's your sense of responsibility?' Alex spoke through gritted teeth, keeping his voice down with difficulty.

'Look, Maud was very distressed and I was busy with Henry,' Elyn hissed back, wishing she didn't sound so defensive. She should have kept a closer eye on her bag, but Alex didn't realise what pressures she had been under. 'Henry was on the verge of going into heart failure and after I'd given him the camoquin injection, Maud and I were getting him into the Land Rover with ice-packs while Tim packed up the tent and all their gear. I suppose he picked up my bag as well.'

'My God, but you're naive,' Alex grated. 'However, this is neither the time nor the place to discuss—' he broke off, as Maud hurried over, anxiety and relief fighting for possession of her plump features.

'Oh, Alex, she's a real treasure,' Maud patted Elyn's arm, a new respect for Elyn glowing in her bright button eyes. 'She was marvellous, she saved Henry's life.' She turned to Elyn, 'If you hadn't come when you did—'

'You had already coped beautifully, Maud,' Elyn reassured her, embarrassed by the extravagant praise, especially after Alex's crushing criticism. Alex was re-straining his impatience with some difficulty and Maud sensed the tension between them.

'I hate to be even more of a nuisance when you're already so busy, but is there somewhere I could have a wash and perhaps make a cup of tea?' She attempted a smile, but Elyn could see that beneath the brave exterior, Maud was just about all in.

'You must stay with me in my bungalow,' Elyn said quickly. 'It's a bit small, but if you can put up with squashed sleeping arrangements, I'd love to have you.'

'Oh, I don't want to put you to any trouble, you've already got enough—'

Elyn raised a hand to stem the tide of words. 'It's no trouble at all,' she said sincerely. 'You and Henry were so kind to me when we first met. You put me at my ease, and made me feel less of a stranger in a strange land.' She resisted a strong temptation to hurl an accusing glare at Alex. Touching Maud's shoulder she pointed to Henry's sleeping figure.

'You'll be able to see your husband as often as you like. In fact, you'll have to help nurse him.' Elyn glanced at Alex for confirmation and he nodded imperceptibly. 'You can see, we're very busy at the moment and we need every pair of hands.'

Maud squared her shoulders and her chest visibly expanded beneath the orange shirt. 'Well, of course, if I can be useful—' She gave a sudden conspiratorial grin. 'This isn't at all like hospitals back in England, is it?'

This time Elyn couldn't resist catching Alex's eye and they exchanged wry smiles that for once were in total accord.

'It certainly isn't,' they agreed in unison.

'Well, I'll go and get my things from the Land Rover,' Maud announced, giving her husband one last loving glance. 'He will be all right?' She couldn't hide the anxiety that hovered just below the surface, a constant, threatening companion.

'He'll be fine,' Elyn promised. 'Here's my key. Make yourself completely at home. Nefra, the maid, will be preparing the evening meal. Just tell her I sent you.'

Maud nodded gratefully. 'Thank you again, both of you,' she said with quiet intensity. 'If anything had happened—you see without Henry—well, I just—' her chin wobbled and she broke off, sudden tears glistening.

Sniffing loudly she threw Elyn a grin. 'This is getting to be a habit, you and me sharing a room!' then stumped off down the ward.

Alex looked at Elyn, his forehead puckering in a puzzled frown as pink tinged Elyn's cheeks.

'I think you'd better come to my office,' he said grimly, 'I've things to say to you that would be better said in private.'

Elyn quailed. He's going to have another go at me about Tim, and all my other faults and I can't take any more, not today, not now.

'I'm afraid I'm behind with my work because of Maud's SOS,' her level tone denied the fear and longing that surged within her at the thought of being alone with him. 'There's still Ali's dressing to change, I don't want to leave it to the nurses just yet, and he needs another injection. Jehan says he's very restless and his temperature is climbing, so if you don't mind, I think we'd better postpone a meeting—'

Alex stared down at her, unmoving, his inscrutable gaze holding her, seeming to reach into the depths of her soul, stripping it bare to reveal her innermost secrets.

With a supreme effort Elyn deliberately turned her head away. Acutely aware of her flaming cheeks she looked across the ward at Ali.

'In my opinion he ought to come off morphine,' she strove for professional coolness, 'he was given an injection on admission and a further one after the op.'

'What alternative had you in mind?' Alex's voice was deep and soft, almost caressing, and while it brought goosebumps up on her arms Elyn was shocked to hear a note of laughter in it. She could still feel his eyes on her, though her own gaze rested everywhere but on him.

'Omnopon,' she answered clearly. Her heart thumped unevenly, so loud that he must surely hear it. Would it amuse him even more, this hopeless love she was trying so desperately to conceal? Or would scorn harden that chiselled face, lift a cynical eyebrow and twist a sneer on those sensual lips?

'It's almost as strong as morphine,' Elyn rushed on, fleeing from her clamorous thoughts, 'but is less likely to cause vomiting or depression of the cough reflex, and of course the addiction risk—' Her voice dried up. He would know all that, she was babbling.

The urge to meet his eyes, to surrender the fight and let him read the naked truth, was dangerously strong. She felt suspended in time and space, as though the busy ward in which they stood face to face, so close that if she swayed just a fraction forward, her body would touch his, had receded. They were alone, free of all weariness, pressure, fear and misunderstanding.

'I'll see to it.' His quiet words jolted her back to reality. 'You go and check that Maud is all right. She puts on a brave face, but this is the second recurrence Henry has had this year and it has shaken her badly.'

'If you're sure you don't need me on—' Elyn began hesitantly.

'I'm sure,' came the firm answer.

Elyn flinched. He couldn't make it more plain. He had no use for her as a doctor or as a woman.

'Have a meal and get freshened up,' he ordered, as if she were a child, 'I want to speak to you later.'

Tight-lipped, she nodded and turned to go, then remembered: 'Jehan put the drug in the nurse's cubicle, I ordered one-third of a grain.'

'Right, I'll deal with it now.'

They walked down the ward together, Elyn painfully conscious of the tall, lean man so close behind her.

'On the—' she began, indicating the tray on the dressing trolley. The tray was empty. Elyn rubbed her hand wearily across her eyes. Surely Jehan had said— but the phial wasn't there, nor was the syringe and distilled water.

'I must have misunderstood,' she shook her head. 'Jehan can't have been to the pharmacy yet. She hasn't brought my keys back. She must be there now. I'll go and—'

'You'll go home, you're not fit to be on the ward. I've

said I'll deal with it, now get along.' Elyn heard only Alex's blunt command. She did not see the compassion that softened his craggy features. Not daring to look up, she hurried from the ward, head down to hide the scalding tears of fatigue and mortification.

What on earth did he expect her to look like after the day she'd had? It was easy enough to look glamorous if you did nothing but flit about in your own plane, visiting people who worked for a living in jobs where caring for people was more important than fashionable clothes or expensive hairdo's.

Elyn stumbled into her bungalow, slammed the door shut and leaned against it with her eyes closed, trying to regain her composure before facing Maud.

A small sound made her jump and her eyes flew open. Maud stood in the tiny sitting room, poised in the act of shaking out a vividly patterned silk dressing gown from her battered suitcase open on the floor. Her face was pink and shiny from the shower and her frizzy hair stuck up in wiry curls all over her head. She wore a pair of voluminous cotton pyjamas in shocking pink.

'What is it, dear? It's not Henry—?'

Elyn shook her head wearily, 'No, he's resting quietly, Maud. He's fine, really.'

'Then, what's the matter? You look right peaky.'

Maud's too-keen eye, and genuine concern in the midst of her own anxiety were too much for Elyn. She covered her face with her hands as the pressures of the previous few days overwhelmed her, snapping the last fragile thread of control.

'Oh, Maud, he's an absolute pig. I hate him.' The words were muffled, but uttered with such force that Maud's eyebrows disappeared into her hair.

'Who, dear? You can't mean Alex?' she said in shocked disbelief.

'Oh can't I? Well I do,' Elyn cried defiantly, scrubbing her tear-streaked face with a fist, and pushing herself away from the door she marched past Maud into the kitchen.

'He's the most arrogant, sarcastic, self-opinionated boor I've ever had the misfortune to meet, let alone work for,' Elyn was trembling with indignation.

'Then why do you?' Maud asked gently, fastening the silk dressing gown around her bulky figure as she followed Elyn into the kitchen.

Ignoring a wide-eyed Nefra who tried to make herself invisible while she continued preparing the meal, Elyn angrily sloshed iced orange-juice into a glass.

'Why do I what?' she snapped as she wiped up the splashes and flung the cloth into the sink.

'Work for him,' Maud said reasonably. 'You aren't bound to stay, my dear. You said yourself he expected a man, so I'm sure the contract could be ignored. Besides, I know this country, the heat, the dust, and diseases we've never heard of back at home. It can't be easy for you, working in a place like this after the kind of hospital you were used to in England.'

'Oh, but I love the work,' Elyn cried hastily, twisting the glass of juice between her palms. 'It's a constant challenge. I don't think I've ever been so tired in my life, but neither have I felt so—so stretched, so alive. But it's him,' the words burst out, 'Maud, he's impossible.'

Maud tied the sash into a floppy bow and led an unresisting Elyn out of the kitchen into the sitting room and pushed her gently into a chair.

'Now, what's he done that's got you all upset like this?' she coaxed, settling herself in the other chair.

Sprawling her long slim legs in front of her, Elyn leaned her head back wearily and gazed at the contents of the glass as she rested it on the chair arm.

How could she tell Maud the truth, that she had fallen totally in love with a man who, professionally, tolerated her only out of necessity, who seemed to make a point of humiliating her at every possible opportunity, and was completely uninterested in her as a woman. No, what little pride she had left forbade it.

'Maud, what's a man like him doing out here?' Elyn cried in bewilderment, fixing her companion with sapphire eyes dark with newly acquired shadows. 'He's a brilliant surgeon, he could be making a fortune in America. Why is he out in this clinic where he can rarely get to use his special talents?'

Maud brushed a hand across the knees of her creased pyjamas, using the movement to gain a little time as she chose her words.

'Why does anyone come to a place like this? People might wonder what brought a pretty young thing like you out here. Folks jump to conclusions, and they might be right, but that's never the whole of the story.'

'Are you trying to tell me—' Elyn sat up, drawing her legs under her, her throat was suddenly dry. She swallowed some juice and noticed that her hand trembled slightly. Lowering the glass, she wrapped both hands round it as she met Maud's thoughtful gaze.

'Was it a broken love affair that brought Alex Davidson to Khalifa?'

'Not in the sense that you mean, dear,' Maud said carefully. 'Alex told Henry quite a long time ago that he thought in the highly-developed countries like Britain and America too much emphasis was being placed on technology in Medicine. He said that while many new developments were beneficial and had a useful role to play, there was a danger of them becoming more important than the patients they were supposed to treat. He felt that the balance was becoming distorted, with doctors needing to know as much about engineering as about anatomy.'

Elyn leaned forward, open-mouthed. 'That's exactly how I felt—' she began, 'and the dangerous reliance on newer and stronger drugs, their unexpected side-effects—'

Maud put a plump finger to her lips.

'Oh Maud, I'm so sorry,' Elyn sank back in her chair. 'It's just that I had no idea—he's never said—please go on.'

'Alex was called in to do an emergency operation one night. He shouldn't have been asked under the circumstances, but there was no-one else with his skill available. The patient had been in a car accident and had a fractured skull. There was bleeding inside the brain.' Maud frowned as she tried to remember the precise details, and Elyn felt herself caught up in the dramatic story.

'Alex's chief insisted they used a new machine, some kind of laser beam for sealing blood vessels. It had only recently been bought by the hospital despite a great hoo-ha over its cost and actual usefulness. Anyway, something went wrong with the machine, there was a power surge or something,' Maud shrugged helplessly, 'the patient died. Of course, she might have died anyway, Alex was quite prepared to admit that.' Maud's face took on a faraway expression.

'It was such a tragedy. She had so much to live for. She was only twenty-three, beautiful, wealthy, you know, one of those society ladies you read about in the gossip columns,' she shook her head sadly.

As Elyn listened she sensed that what she was hearing was of vital importance, and yet a sudden fear of knowing more gripped her, a gnawing unease that dried her mouth and dampened the palms of her hands. Yet she could not bring herself to stop Maud and the older woman went on.

'Afterwards, Alex said he couldn't stay in England and he didn't want to go to the States or anywhere else where hospital politics were held to be more important than a surgeon's skill or a patient's life,' Maud sighed. 'That's when he applied to the World Health Organisation for a pioneer clinic post, and they sent him here.'

Elyn's heart ached for the man she loved. 'I can imagine how he must have felt. Losing a patient is something you never get used to. I remember my first. She was seventy and had tripped over her hall rug and broken her hip. Luckily a neighbour found her soon after it happened and she was in hospital within an hour. I was on orthopaedic rotation and assisted at the operation to pin the fracture. She came through the op.

beautifully,' Elyn smiled at the memory, 'and the day after she was as chirpy as a cricket.' Her smile faded. 'That night she died. Pulmonary embolism.'

Elyn rubbed her hand across her eyes. 'I know she was old and death occurs quite frequently after a fall resulting in a broken bone. Then there's the shock to the system of the actual operation—' she shook her head. 'But I couldn't accept it. I kept thinking it was our fault, that if we'd done something different, if we'd somehow done more, she wouldn't have died.'

She shrugged wearily and Maud nodded her understanding. 'It's one of the hardest things for a doctor to face.' Elyn pressed the cool glass against her cheek. 'Obviously for a specialist surgeon who is dealing with critically ill patients all the time, the risk is much higher. But for a surgeon of Alex's experience to have walked out on his career because of what happened—' she ran her fingers through her tumbled curls, aware of a twinge of guilt at discussing her superior this way. But she could not separate the man from the doctor. There was so much about him she did not understand and she was hungry for any snippet of information which could provide a glimpse of yet another facet of the complex personality of the man to whom she was drawn as helplessly as a moth to a flame.

'Don't judge him harshly, dear,' Maud chided gently, 'I told you it wasn't a simple decision. You see, the woman who died while he was operating—'

Elyn had a sudden appalling premonition of what was coming. She opened her mouth and Maud hesitated, shocked by Elyn's pallor, but before Elyn could speak, Maud finished quietly, 'they were engaged to be married.'

Elyn's eyes closed as pain hacked at her like jagged glass. The tiny bud of hope, nourished by her dreams that somehow, someday, he might feel as she did, that the kisses which stirred her to the depths of her being might also mean something to him, in that moment died.

Now so much was clear. He must have been totally devastated, his broken heart refusing all consolation save the challenge of establishing the clinic and winning the trust and confidence of the people. His supreme success was a measure of his dedication.

Until Samina, wealthy, beautiful, socialite Samina. A dusky version of the girl who had died. The girl he had loved. Fate was offering him a second chance, not only at love but also to resume his brilliant career. For surely, judging by the fact that Samina piloted her own plane, money was no object and her father's private clinic in Cairo would be a far cry from the one here at Khalifa.

Recalling Alex's casual, almost irritated attitude to Samina, a doubt crept into Elyn's mind, but she dismissed it with a sigh as mere wishful thinking. He was not a man to wear his heart on his sleeve, that much Elyn did know. Besides, hadn't she seen them both locked in a passionate embrace only yesterday?

Elyn clenched her fists. How would she bear it?

'My dear girl, are you all right?' Maud was deeply concerned. 'What ever is it? Did I say something—?'

Elyn made a supreme effort. The poor woman had been through enough already. It was totally unfair to add to her worries. She opened her eyes and pulled her face into a smile, though the muscles of her face were stiff and aching with the effort of not weeping.

'Sorry, Maud. I'm just very tired. We've been rushed off our feet the last few days and I think it's hit me all at once.' Pulling herself to her feet, she carefully placed the glass on the table. 'I think I'll go and get a shower—' her voice faltered and she gritted her teeth. She would not break down, she would *not*.

'You do look exhausted,' Maud agreed, tutting, as she eyed Elyn critically, 'and I think you've lost a bit of weight. I hope Alex isn't driving you too hard. He forgets that not everybody has his stamina. Look, you go and have a nice shower and I'll get us a cup of tea, I think we could both do with one.'

Elyn nodded, not trusting herself to speak. Just as she was about to cross the narrow passage to her room, there came a knock on the door. The firm rap-rap was so characteristic that Elyn knew instantly who it was. She spun round to Maud, too tired, too unhappy to pretend any longer.

'Please—you answer it. I can't.'

Maud's eyebrows rose in surprise. 'But—I expect it's only Alex come to make sure I've settled in. He's so thoughtful—'

'I know it's Alex,' Elyn whispered desperately, 'and I can't see him Maud, not at the moment, not until—' She twisted her fingers together. 'I can't explain—' her eyes, huge and overbright, pleaded.

Maud studied her for a few seconds, while another tattoo beat on the door, making Elyn jump. She glanced anxiously at the door and back at Maud. 'Please—' she begged.

'You don't have to explain anything, dear,' Maud touched her arm gently, a knowing smile creasing her face. 'Such anger—I should have guessed,' she added shrewdly. 'Don't worry now, he'll learn nothing from me. You nip into the shower, and if he wants to speak to you, I'll explain you're busy.'

Whispering heartfelt thanks, Elyn darted into the tiny bathroom and turned on the shower tap full blast as she stripped off her dust-stained clothes. She stepped under the shower and the hissing needles of cold water on her face and head cut out all other sound.

She didn't want to hear Alex's voice, for if he spoke of her at all, she knew it would be in disparagement.

In fact the exchange between Alex and Maud, though brief, was highly significant, and as Maud closed the door on the departing man, her plump, rosy face wore an expression of mingled exasperation and wistfulness.

The following day the crowded wards kept both doctors busy until late in the morning.

Elyn entered Alex's office with her arms full of reports. She had just sent the nurse who had accompanied her on rounds back to her duties when Jehan bustled in with two cups of coffee.

'Is one of those yours, Jehan?' Elyn asked hopefully as she dumped the folders on the already crowded desk.

Jehan shook her head, 'No, *hanem*, Dr Davidson ask me to make for you both as soon as you finish ward rounds.'

Elyn's stomach tightened in wary anticipation. So Alex was determined on confrontation, and there seemed no way she could avoid him. At least she felt more equal to the challenge today. After her shower last night, she had emerged from her room to join Maud in the sitting room for the promised cup of tea, wondering nervously how she would handle the questions which had been almost visibly bubbling on Maud's lips after her reaction to Alex's knock.

But to her surprise Maud did not once refer to him, except to say that, as she guessed, he had called to make sure she was all right, and to tell her that Henry was resting quietly. Then she had briskly changed the subject, asking about Elyn's family.

Though in one sense vastly relieved, Elyn had to suppress a slight disappointment. She had never before confided in anyone. Though she loved her father and he loved her, he was a remote figure, almost completely engrossed in his research. Losing her mother at an early age had placed an additional restraint on her innate shyness. Though she loved her aunt and was deeply grateful for her kindness, Elyn had not wished to burden her or anyone else with problems or decisions she felt were her responsibility.

But Maud was different, so open and warm-hearted, and, Elyn instinctively sensed, completely trustworthy. What a blessed relief it would have been to have poured out all her confusion and misery. Not that she expected Maud to provide a solution, there was none, Elyn was only too aware of that, but how it would have helped to

simply have unburdened herself of the secret which
touched every part of her life and weighed so heavily on
her heart.

But Maud appeared to have forgotten the minutes
before Alex's arrival, Elyn's near-betrayal of her feelings and her own shrewd guess. Or perhaps, Elyn admitted, Maud just wasn't interested, having more than
enough problems of her own to cope with.

They spent a pleasant evening lingering over the
delicious meal Nefra had prepared. Maud monopolised
the conversation and in spite of her mental and physical
exhaustion, Elyn had been enthralled by the stories of
tours, excavations and archaeological digs Maud and
Henry had undertaken, and the breathtaking and often
hilarious incidents which had occurred.

Maud had packed her off to bed just after ten, and
despite her unspoken fears of a sleepless night, Elyn lost
consciousness almost as her head hit the pillow. She
awoke eight hours later, more refreshed than for several
days.

Sinking gratefully into the chair, Elyn lifted a cup
from the tray, sipped the aromatic coffee, and tried to
relax, making the most of the few precious seconds she
had to herself.

She had almost finished her coffee when Alex walked
in, acknowledging her presence with a brief nod.
Though she managed to maintain her outward composure, her heart lurched.

His crisp whites accentuated the mahogany tan that
darkened his face, neck and arms. Was he that colour all
over, Elyn wondered, and a mental image of his lean,
muscular body, stripped to the waist and gleaming with
sweat, as she had once glimpsed him in the changing
room, brought a rush of blood to her cheeks. His black
hair was, as usual, slightly rumpled. But even as she
looked quickly away, concentrating on the coffee
grounds in the bottom of her cup, it was the aura of
powerful, almost aggressive masculinity which surrounded him, of which he was either unconscious or

uncaring, that set Elyn's blood pounding and tautened her nerves.

He pulled his stethoscope from his neck and pushed it into his tunic pocket. Then, perching himself on the corner of the desk nearest to Elyn, he picked up his coffee and took a swallow, grimacing.

'Better luke-warm than stone cold, I suppose,' he remarked, half-smiling, and set the cup down, clasping his hands and resting them on his raised knee.

'There are several things I want to talk to you about,' he said slowly, almost diffidently, looking directly into Elyn's eyes. She found it difficult to breathe. She leaned forward to set her cup back on the tray. He took it from her absently and his fingers brushed hers. Elyn jumped as the touch sent tiny flames shooting up her arm and warmth suffused her body, bringing a glow to her skin. She quickly disguised the involuntary start by shifting her position on the chair, but not before she had been surprised by the startled expression in his own eyes, swiftly masked, but undeniable. There was no time to wonder what it meant.

'Look,' Alex ran his fingers through his hair, rumpling it even more, 'about Tim Preston—'

'Oh no,' Elyn murmured softly. 'Look,' she broke in, 'surely enough has been said, you made yourself quite clear.'

Alex's face stiffened imperceptibly. 'I don't think you understand,' he said patiently, 'there's something about him you obviously haven't grasped. I'll be kind and put it down to inexperience—'

'Oh, will you?' Elyn shot back, angry colour flooding her face like a tide, 'you should make up your mind. When we were caught in the sandstorm you practically accused me of being a harlot!'

Puzzlement creased Alex's forehead, only to be replaced by amusement as realisation dawned. 'On that aspect of your character, I assure you there are no doubts in my mind as to the true situation. However, that is not what I was referring to.'

Elyn looked down quickly. Agonising embarrassment burned from her hair to her toes. If only the floor would open up and swallow her. Above the normal sounds of the clinic Elyn heard the faint drone of an engine growing louder. Alex made no reference to it and so absorbed was she in her own thoughts that its significance didn't register. Goaded by emotions she did not understand, Elyn leapt to her feet and grasped the back of her chair. Eyes flashing, she turned to Alex.

'Look, you've made it plain you don't care for Tim Preston, but you aren't above using him when it suits you. It was your idea that he met me at Cairo Airport when you were too busy,' there was more than a touch of sarcasm in Elyn's tone. 'Just because I don't share your dislike of him, the reason for which you have not seen fit to share with me—'

Alex's face darkened. Anger tightened his mouth and he threw up his hands in exasperation.

'It has nothing to do with liking or disliking—'

But Elyn, driven by what she saw as injustice, coupled with her own over-strained emotions, would not let him finish.

'I did not invite Tim to the clinic yesterday. I have had neither the time nor the energy for social calls since I arrived here, but if he hadn't come, Henry Barnes might well have died.'

'I accept that,' Alex grated, 'but that's not important right now. What I'm trying, with great difficulty, to get through to you is that under no circumstances is Preston to set foot in this clinic again. Nor are you to—'

'This is too much,' Elyn exploded, glaring at him. 'As Director and Senior Doctor of this clinic, your rules on medical matters I'll accept without question, but you have absolutely no rights over my personal—'

In one panther-like spring, Alex was off the desk towering over her. He grasped her shoulders, his strong fingers biting into her flesh, and shook her. Elyn's head wobbled like a blossom too heavy for its stem. She gasped, every nerve tingling with icy fire at his touch, and her knees turned to water.

'You little fool,' he blazed, 'this *is* a medical matter. For God's sake, Elyn, are you blind? Don't you recognise the signs? Can't you see he's a—'

A commotion outside the door into the passage cut him short. Jehan's voice raised in protest brought a growl of fury from Alex and he abruptly released Elyn who staggered against the desk, desperately trying to calm her ragged breathing and regain her shaken control.

Alex had taken one stride towards the door when a throaty female voice cut across that of the Chief Nurse.

'You run along back to your bedpans and your patients. Dr Davidson never minds *me* disturbing him—'

The door opened and Samina whirled in on a cloud of exotic perfume. She was vibrant in a short-sleeved flying suit of coral linen. Her low-heeled sandals matched perfectly and her hair, parted in the centre, swung loose, a rippling, ebony curtain. In the starkly, clinical office, she shimmered like a bird of paradise.

Rubbing her upper arms where Alex's steely grip had bruised them, Elyn could not escape the vivid memory of the last time she had seen Samina. The Egyptian had been locked in Alex's arms.

The image brought a knifing pain, and as she turned away from Samina fearing the Egyptian might perceive the tumult within her, Elyn glimpsed Alex's face.

His expression was stony, his mouth compressed in a thin line and his eyes glinted dangerously.

There was no word of welcome just a cold, terse, 'Well?'

Elyn was utterly confused.

'Darling Alex,' Samina gushed, 'I know I've broken my promise, but you'll forgive me,' she flashed a glance at Elyn, whose heart was racing, partly because of the interrupted scene with Alex, but partly because of the malicious glee sparkling in Samina's dark eyes, in vivid contrast to her innocent expression.

'I've brought a present, a special gift,' she slipped her arm through Alex's and kissed him lightly on the cheek, pressing her voluptuous body against his as she did so. She appeared not to notice when he deliberately moved away.

'Actually, it is for your little assistant,' she turned khol-lined eyes on Elyn, who was shocked and bewildered by the venom in them.

'If your staff is happy, then you are happy. Is that not so, my sweet?' The smile she gave Alex had a hard edge to it.

'Let's get this farce over with, Samina,' Alex's voice was glacial. 'Go and get whatever it is, we have work to do.'

'Patience, darling,' she gurgled. 'You don't have to wait a moment longer.' She turned to the door which she had left ajar and with barely suppressed excitement flung it open, calling, 'You can come in now.'

As Elyn saw who stood on the threshold, her head spun and the room tilted crazily around her. 'Mike,' she gasped, feeling the blood drain from her face, 'what on earth are you doing here?'

'Elyn, darling,' he exclaimed in passionate tones, and ignoring Alex completely, he strode across the room. 'Thank God, I've found you at last.'

Before Elyn could move, he had pulled her into his arms and she found herself trapped in a crushing embrace as he rained kisses on her face and neck.

CHAPTER SEVEN

STUNNED and speechless, Elyn looked over Mike's shoulder straight into the bleak face of Alex Davidson. His glacial expression forced a wordless cry from Elyn as she struggled desperately to free herself.

'Come, Alex,' Samina said archly, 'we should leave the love-birds together.'

'No,' Elyn cried sharply, fighting clear of Mike's arms at last. She took a quick step backwards as he advanced on her once more.

'Elyn, precious,' he cajoled.

Elyn glimpsed smug satisfaction spreading cat-like across Samina's beautiful face. Turning to Alex, she was chilled by his icy disdain.

'Your personal affairs are becoming something of a liability to this clinic,' he remarked, each word a barb in Elyn's flesh. 'You and your—' he paused, 'your friend obviously have unfinished business to discuss. You may have the use of this office for five minutes. After which, I must insist you return to your duties.'

'No,' Elyn repeated breathlessly, 'it's not necessary. We have nothing to—'

'Sweetheart,' Mike broke in reproachfully, 'don't be so ungracious.' He slipped his arm around her waist.

Alex, his hand on the door handle, glanced from Mike to Elyn. 'Five minutes,' he repeated coldly, and, sweeping Samina ahead of him, walked out, closing the door firmly behind him.

Elyn spun round, wrenching herself free, and slapped Mike's hand away.

'Let go of me,' she hissed, her eyes blazing with anger. 'How dare you! What the hell do you think you're doing, barging in here, interrupting my work, and behaving like—like some second-rate movie actor!'

'Elyn, honey,' Mike began, adopting a conciliatory tone, 'aren't you glad I'm here? God, it's wonderful to see you again.'

'No, I'm not glad to see you,' Elyn shouted at him. 'What made you think I would be? Our engagement is over, finished. You broke it off, remember? You had found someone who was more fun to be with. So where is *she* now? Surely she hasn't come with you.'

Mike was obviously taken aback by Elyn's uncharacteristic forcefulness. At the mention of the broken engagement he shifted uncomfortably, rubbing his ear as he turned all his charm on Elyn.

'I don't blame you for being cross,' he said generously. 'But I couldn't miss this chance of us getting together again. You see, I realise what a fool I've been, how wrong I was to let you go.'

'You didn't let me go, Mike,' Elyn said calmly, 'you threw me over, for someone else, someone—gay and frivolous, someone with whom you had fallen in love.' Elyn gazed levelly at him, feeling a warm glow of satisfaction at his obvious discomfort and at her own ability to cope with this dreadful scene that had been forced upon her without a hint of warning.

'Well, Mike, where is she?'

Mike shrugged impatiently, 'Who knows? I left her in New York, she decided to stay on with friends when I returned to London. Of course, by then I realised what a fool I'd been and how much I missed you. Oh, Elyn—'

'Stay where you are,' Elyn ordered. 'Don't come one step nearer or I'll—you'll be sorry. Anyway, how did you find out where I was?'

Mike shoved his hands into his trouser pockets and leaned nonchalantly against the filing cabinet.

'The drug company I work for has been expanding its markets and we wanted to establish an opening in the Middle East. I was sent out to Cairo and as well as contacting the big hospitals I was approaching smaller nursing homes and private clinics. I got an appointment to see Mr Youssef and met Samina.' He shrugged. 'She mentioned the clinic here and when she described the young lady doctor fresh out from England, well, I knew it just had to be you.'

'I can't imagine Samina describing me in terms anyone would recognise,' Elyn murmured drily. 'I'm surprised she put herself to the trouble of flying you out here.'

'She couldn't have been more helpful,' Mike said ingenuously, 'once she knew we'd been engaged, she insisted on bringing me. Of course, I told her what an idiot I'd been,' he added hastily. 'She said she would love to be the fairy godmother who brought us together again.'

'Witch, more like,' Elyn muttered. 'Well, she's going to be disappointed,' she said firmly, 'because you've both had a wasted journey.'

Mike was astonished. 'You can't mean it, Elyn.'

'Oh, I can, and I do.'

'But I've come all this way—I mean, I've said I'm sorry.'

'No, you haven't, Mike. But it doesn't matter.'

'You mean you won't take me back?' His disbelief was so open and so real Elyn had to suppress a smile.

'No, Mike, I won't. Did you honestly expect that I would?' She could hardly credit his ego. To him it had appeared quite simple. Butter Elyn up a bit, act contrite and she'll fall like a ripe plum. Anger stirred again in her. How little he really thought of her. This whole thing was no more than a sop to his bruised pride. How dare he think she was so gullible? Then she remembered. She had been exactly that. He had tossed her lies and excuses and she had believed them, swallowed them whole, never thought to question or wonder at his prolonged trips abroad, his late business meetings, the times when his secretary had offered a dozen smooth reasons for his absence.

No, Elyn allowed, the fault was not entirely Mike's. She *had* been gullible. If that's what it meant to trust someone and believe what they had told you. Only she hadn't called it gullibility, she had thought it was love.

Now she could see him for what he was, vain, charming and utterly self-centred.

'So, it's all over between us, then?' a hard note crept into his voice.

'It was over a long time ago, Mike,' Elyn replied calmly. It gave her no pleasure to turn the tables on him, she felt only sadness that they had both been so blind and wasted each others' time.

'Who is he, then?' Mike demanded harshly.

'Who's what? What are you talking about?' Elyn was bewildered.

'The new boyfriend, what else?' Mike said impatiently.

'There is no new boyfriend,' Elyn replied, hanging on to her composure, keeping her voice level with some effort.

'Oh, come on now, don't try to fool me. Dedicated you might be but you're also human; flesh and blood, warm flesh and hot blood if I remember correctly,' his mouth twisted in a lascivious grin.

'Don't be unpleasant, Mike.' Elyn could feel unease growing. She had underestimated the blow to his pride. Surely he wasn't going to resort to crude innuendo and nastiness to hit back at her. 'I think you'd better go. Dr Davidson——'

'Of course,' he slapped his forehead and turned on her, sneering accusation distorting his features. 'I should have realised, the good doctor. He's king rat on this particular dung heap.' Mike was deliberately scornful. 'I knew there had to be some reason for you burying yourself out here. I thought you were carrying a torch for me. Still, if you pull it off with Saint Alex, you'll have done quite well for yourself, Elyn. I hear he was quite a good surgeon, once.'

Fury gripped Elyn, but she held it tightly under control for she was aware of time running out. The five minutes Alex had allowed her must be up. Someone could come for her at any moment. But first she had to convince Mike that there was nothing between her and

Alex Davidson. For Mike's jealousy and bitterness might easily prompt him to make some snide remark to Alex that could undermine and destroy the facade of feigned indifference she had so carefully maintained.

'Let's get things straight once and for all, Mike.' Elyn fought down her temper. 'I am here because I like the work. I did not come out to Egypt on the rebound from you, I came to develop my skills as a doctor.' Elyn edged towards the door. 'I have the greatest admiration and respect for Alex Davidson as a doctor, and, for your information, he is still a brilliant surgeon. However, there is not and never has been anything more than a professional relationship between us.'

Elyn swallowed painfully as she uttered the lie. But it wasn't wholly a lie. It was true for Alex. As for her—she was suddenly overwhelmed by vivid memories of those timeless moments in the Land Rover when wind and sand had become a living hell of dust and heat and noise. When Alex's arms and lips had transported her out of her terror into another world, a world of searing emotions and quivering sensuality. And again, in this very office, when he had used his superior strength to crush her body to his, and had taken her lips cruelly, mercilessly, draining her of all strength and of the will to resist.

'You expect me to believe that?' Mike sneered.

'I don't give a damn what you believe,' Elyn cried, 'but I'll tell you this,' reckless, angry, wanting only to be rid of him, she glared at Mike, aware only of the hurt and confusion seething inside her, 'for self-satisfaction, arrogance and overblown ego, there's precious little to choose between you and Alex Davidson.' A spiteful smile tilted the corners of Mike's weak mouth. 'And I wouldn't touch either of you with a ten-foot pole.' Elyn's eyes flashed. 'Now get out of here.' She swung round to wrench open the door and thumped straight into Alex.

Her breath caught on a gasp and for the second time that day, Elyn wished the floor would open beneath her feet. A crimson tide flooded her throat and face and she broke out in a dew of perspiration that turned icy beneath the cynical green gaze.

How long had he been standing there? Why had he had to hear those last words? She swayed and pushed against him in an effort to flee, but his hand imprisoned her arm against his chest and the grip was so firm, so strong, that she knew it was useless to struggle, and with Mike behind her, unaware of Alex's clasp, she could not even try.

Mike must have seen Alex come in, must have known he was there behind her. Yet instead of saying something, warning her, he had let her rant on, and had enjoyed every second of the terrible scene.

Elyn closed her eyes. How could she ever look Alex in the face again? She couldn't possibly tell him she'd only said those things to put Mike off the scent, to hide the truth of *her* feelings. What a dreadful mess she'd made of everything.

'The lady certainly doesn't appear to hold either of us in very high regard,' Mike sniggered archly at Alex.

'The lady asked you to leave,' Alex's icy quietness was to Elyn an unmistakable sign of his anger. Fear shivered through her, while her hand, caught against his chest in a grip of steel, burned, as through the thin cotton tunic she felt his strong steady heartbeat.

'I'm going, I'm going,' Mike said airily, walking towards the door, 'I'm the last person to stay where I'm not wanted.'

'I'm so glad you understand,' Alex was coldly polite. He released Elyn's hand after giving it a warning squeeze, which she interpreted as an instruction not to move.

As Mike picked up the briefcase he had dropped on entering the office, he turned to Alex. 'I don't suppose I could interest you in the new cardiac drug my company has sent me out here to promote?' he began hopefully.

Alex studied him for a moment, his face grimmer than ever. 'Mr—?' he raised an eyebrow.

'Oh, Fernley, Mike Fernley,' Mike switched on his

professional salesman's smile, and thrust out a hand which Alex ignored.

'Well, Mr Fernley,' he drawled, 'had I ever done business with your company before, the arrangement would cease as from this moment. Goodbye.'

If Elyn had not been so wretched, she would have found it hard to suppress a giggle at Mike's double-take before his smile was switched off again and two dull splotches of colour appeared on his cheeks.

'Well, I can't exactly say it's been a pleasure,' he blustered.

'The feeling is mutual. Goodbye,' Alex repeated firmly, relentlessly driving Mike out into the passage. He turned in the doorway. 'Please wait,' he said to Elyn 'we have hospital business to discuss.' His tone was level and pleasant, but Elyn was under no illusion, it was an order, not a request.

Sinking into a chair, Elyn buried her face in her hands as reaction swept through her, leaving her weak and shaking. Her thoughts were chaotic, a kaleidoscope of shock, fear, relief and misery.

A long shuddering sigh welled from the depths of her being. Clasping her hands tightly in her lap, Elyn stared blindly at the wall, opening her eyes very wide to dispel the scalding tears that hovered so perilously near. She took a deep breath, and another. Gradually her control returned. She carefully wiped her eyes with a tissue, she blew her nose, and took another deep breath.

The door opened and Alex re-entered the room, his powerful presence making it seem suddenly smaller.

Elyn had swung round at the sound and now found herself backed against the desk. Alex's expression was inscrutable as his eyes, cool and green and unfathomable as a mountain lake, scanned her face.

Elyn felt the familiar tension building in her again. Still he did not speak, just watched and waited. At last she could bear it no longer.

'I'm sorry,' she burst out.

'Sorry?' Alex drawled, 'for what are you sorry?'

The curious mixture of love and irritation, warmth and frustration he always managed to arouse in her, churned once more. 'For that appalling scene,' Elyn shrugged helplessly.

'Why do you apologise? It was obviously not of your making,' Alex replied reasonably. Elyn breathed a sigh of relief. Too soon.

'However,' he went on, his voice several degrees colder, 'perhaps you would tell me how many more discarded boyfriends are liable to turn up without warning. This is neither a circus nor a marriage bureau.'

Elyn's head snapped up, angry colour scorching her cheeks. A furious retort sprang to her lips, but she bit it back. He had every right to be angry. This was a hospital and sick people's problems took precedence. Apart from the annoyance caused by disruption to an already hectic day, had he not just heard her liken him to Mike, and infer they were both beneath her contempt? If only he knew—

'I can assure you there are no more,' she stated with such quiet force, Alex's quizzical eyebrow lifted lazily.

The sound of an aircraft engine drew her gaze involuntarily to the window. As the drone receded, and Elyn mentally wished the plane and its two occupants a fervent 'good riddance', she looked back quickly, guiltily, to see him still watching her.

Their eyes met, held, and something in his started her heart pounding. He moved towards her, Elyn felt the edge of the desk top pressing into the back of her thighs. His eyes glittered and his expression was hard and cold.

'Tell me,' he growled softly, 'am I really so abhorrent to you?'

Elyn was trapped. Backed against the desk she could not move. He had only to raise either arm to block her escape. But still he moved forward, as smooth and as dangerous as a leopard.

Nor could she speak, for what could she say? How could she look into his eyes and say she hated him? Ye how could she tell him the truth? Either way she was damned.

She lowered her head, desperately seeking an escape. Her long eyelashes, protective fans, shielded her vulnerable eyes from his piercing gaze.

'Look at me, Elyn.' The words were a deep rumble.

She did not, could not move.

His hand came up and cupped her chin, his strong fingers spread along the right side of her jaw, his thumb on the left.

'Look at me,' he repeated, slowly, inexorably tilting her head back. Her throat dry, her heart thudding like a hammer as liquid fire raced along her veins, Elyn lifted her sapphire eyes to his.

She could not escape. She must bluff. Digging her nails into her palms so hard that they pierced the flesh, Elyn met his hooded gaze and knew in a split second she was no match for the man who towered over her.

'Self-satisfied, arrogant, egotistical,' he murmured softly, the little pause between each word giving it greater emphasis, hitting Elyn even harder with the realisation of what she'd done. Her knees turned to water. Only the desk and Alex's steely grip on her chin prevented her collapsing at his feet.

Alex leaned down towards Elyn and her eyes widened in fear.

'So,' he growled, 'you wouldn't touch me with a ten-foot pole.'

A choked sob caught in Elyn's throat as Alex's free arm seized her around the waist, pressing her body against the hard-muscled length of his own.

His eyes glittered and his mouth curved in a slow lazy smile that had a touch of cruelty in it. 'We'll see about that.'

'No,' Elyn breathed, straining with every fibre away from him. 'No, don't.'

He did not deign to reply, but as he brought his head down towards Elyn's pale, upturned face, the door opened and Jehan hurried in. She checked momentarily at the sight of the two doctors apparently clasped in a loving embrace, but, Elyn realised later, she did not appear unduly surprised, in fact there was almost a look of satisfaction on her olive features.

Alex released Elyn with neither undue haste, nor reluctance. Both of them knew that sooner or later he would exact his revenge, and no interruption, long or short, would deter him.

Jehan gave Elyn a quick smile, then turned to Alex. 'Doctor, I am doing ante-natal. Please you come and see Sheikha Leila. The baby has moved, is transverse.' Her face mirrored her concern.

'I'll come at once,' Without a backward glance he followed Jehan out of the office.

The arrival of the Chief Nurse and her reminder of the constant demands of the clinic helped restore Elyn's emotional balance. She knew that, if he chose, within a very short time she would once again be in Alex Davidson's arms. Strangely, her fear had gone. It was as though the situation had been taken out of her hands and was completely beyond her control. There was only fatalistic acceptance. *Insh'allah*, the will of Allah. It was a phrase she heard often in the clinic. Perhaps, Elyn thought pensively, she was becoming more a part of the land and people than she had realised.

Crossing to the wash-stand in the corner, she splashed cold water on her face and rinsed her hands, drying them on a fluffy white towel. Then, raking her fingers through her curls and feeling refreshed, she sat down behind the desk and pulled the pile of folders towards her to begin the never-ending task of updating the patients' notes.

Fifteen minutes later a tentative knock on the office door made Elyn look up. One of the trainees stood diffidently on the threshold.

'Dr Davidson ask for you, *hanem*,' she struggled with heavily-accented English.

Elyn sighed and closed the file in which she was writing. She smiled reassuringly at the young nurse and followed her to the Ante-Natal Clinic near the maternity ward.

As Elyn entered the examination room, she could see Jehan trying very hard, but not very successfully, to hide a smile, while Alex, surprised and impatient, was being soundly berated in a strange tongue Elyn did not recognise as Arabic.

The woman scolding him was tall and draped from head to toe in the characteristic blue veil and cloak of the Tuareg. Her voice was low and musical but held a note of proud authority Elyn had never before encountered in an Arab woman.

'What language is that?' Elyn whispered to Jehan.

'It is Berber dialect, *hanem*,' she murmured in reply. 'Most desert dwellers, the nomads, speak French, but the Tuareg speak their own tongue, Tamashek. Dr Davidson make Magda and I learn it and he learn it himself when the Bedouins begin to settle here in Khalifa. But it is very hard to speak and impossible to write!'

'So is Arabic for some of us,' Elyn smiled back, then moved to join Alex. 'You wished to see me, Dr Davidson?' she said quietly.

Alex turned. 'Yes,' he said briefly. 'The Sheikha requires a second opinion. I have explained that the baby must be turned, but she is upset and anxious.' He added rapidly, 'She miscarried earlier this year and is worried that the manoeuvre will damage the baby in some way.' A sardonic smile curled his mouth. 'She had heard about the new lady doctor and says that a woman will understand her feelings.'

'But I have not had children,' Elyn said quickly.

'Apparently that is not important, the Sheikha insists you examine and advise her.'

As if to confirm his words, the woman leaned forward and lightly touched Elyn's hand. The dark-brown eyes with their fringe of black lashes were raised to Elyn's and she saw, beneath the haughty pride, uncertainty and fear.

Elyn automatically covered the woman's hand with her own and smiled at her.

'Jehan, will you assist and can you translate? I want to explain what I'm doing and why.' She glanced at Alex. 'I'm sure Dr Davidson has already done this but the Sheikha obviously needs more reassurance.'

Alex made no comment, merely indicating that she was to proceed. 'I'll go back to the ward and check on Hamid and Ali.' He glanced at his watch. 'I'll have a look at Henry Barnes too, then I'll be back for your appraisal.'

Elyn could not understand the glint in his eye until Jehan murmured as they prepared the Sheikha on the examination table, 'Dr Davidson, he not explain anything, he just say "don't worry, all is well". This one she demand more. She strong lady.'

Elyn bit her lips on an impish grin. Alex Davidson, celebrated surgeon, was out of his depth in obstetrics, where a woman's emotional well-being was as important as her physical health.

Elyn examined Leila thoroughly, talking slowly and gently all the time, stopping every few minutes to allow Jehan to translate.

Her own shock at her first glimpse of the young woman's face, hands and feet, with their delicate tracery of henna, was soon forgotten. As she strapped the cuff of the spygmomanometer on Leila's arm, Elyn explained the significance of blood pressure and the need, during pregnancy, to keep it down with plenty of rest and a good diet.

She listened to the baby's heart, then put the ear pieces of the stethoscope into Leila's ears. The look of surprise and awe on the expectant mother's face as she listened intently, brought a lump to Elyn's throat.

Leila whispered something and Jehan said, 'She say it is like the wings of a bird.'

Leila spoke again, resting her slim brown hand protectively over her bulging belly, as she looked at Elyn with shining eyes.

'My son is strong, he has the heart of a falcon. I tell his father I have heard it myself,' Jehan translated. She too was obviously touched by the young woman's fierce joy and pride.

Alex re-entered the room quietly, but his presence made an immediate, though different impact on all three women.

'Please tell the Sheikha that Dr Davidson spoke the truth,' Elyn said quickly to Jehan, folding her stethoscope into her tunic pocket. 'She's in her thirty-fifth week and the baby can't engage while it lies across her womb like this. We must turn the baby so that his head is down in the right place for him to be born when the time comes.' Thoughtfully, Elyn draped a sheet over the young woman.

Leila's eyes never left Elyn while Jehan explained and when she had finished Leila rapped out some words that sounded like an order.

'She wish you to do it, *hanem*,' Jehan said.

'Tell her it needs a strong hand and I am not strong enough, but I will stay with her while Dr Davidson does it,' Elyn replied.

After a moment's hesitation, Leila nodded and Alex turned to the Chief Nurse. 'Jehan, will you get a Trilene inhaler from the pharmacy. She'll need light anaesthesia and I don't want to upset her further by hauling in the whole bottle apparatus from the operating theatre.' He crossed the room to wash his hands at the sink in the corner.

Jehan nodded. 'May I have your keys, Doctor?'

Elyn glanced up. 'Haven't you still got mine?'

Jehan was surprised. 'No, *hanem*, I gave them to the pupil helping on men's ward to return them to you. She is outside. One moment, I ask her.' She opened the door into the waiting room and called in the young nurse, who managed to look efficient and nervous at the same time.

'Yesterday I gave Dr Scott's pharmacy keys to you to give to her,' Jehan said.

The pupil nurse nodded.

'Then where are they?' Elyn asked gently, controlling

a spasm of irritation. The keys should have been returned as soon as Jehan had finished with them. Elyn could understand Jehan not bringing them herself, she was always busy, and yesterday had been particularly hectic, with the admission of the extra bilharzia patients and Henry Barnes. Even she had forgotten about them until now.

The girl glanced wide-eyed at the two doctors and Chief Nurse in turn. 'I gave keys to Mr Preston,' she blurted.

Elyn's head jerked up.

'You did what?' Alex's face was terrifying, though his voice barely rose above a whisper.

The pupil twisted her hands together in front of her. She was on the verge of tears as her eyes darted between the three shocked faces staring at her.

'I gave them to Mr Preston,' she repeated.

'But why?' Jehan demanded.

'He said it was Dr Scott's order. I was to give him the pharmacy keys and he would return them to her. He said Dr Scott ask him to fetch something from pharmacy.'

The words spilled from her trembling lips in a mixture of Arabic and English. But there was no doubting the meaning of what she said, and Elyn felt herself growing numb with shock.

'I did not want to do it, but he said it was an order from Dr Scott.' The girl pleaded with each in turn, 'How could I disobey?'

Jehan glanced at Alex and he jerked his head briefly. 'All right, you may return to your duties,' Jehan said briskly, 'do not speak of this to anyone. It is simply a misunderstanding, do you understand?'

The young nurse gulped and nodded quickly, then scuttled out of the examination room.

Alex tossed Jehan his keys, 'The Trilene inhaler, please,' and she too hurried out, aware of the crackling tension in the room.

Elyn was too stunned to think coherently. 'Why?' she whispered, gazing disbelievingly at Alex.

'You did not send him for your keys?' Alex rapped out.

'Do I have to deny it?' Elyn flung back hotly. 'Do you think I don't know better than that?'

'Attend to your patient,' Alex snapped brusquely. 'We'll discuss it later.'

Elyn blinked at the sharpness in his face and expression. But it helped her recover, and she turned to Leila who was struggling to sit up on the couch, obviously aware something was wrong. Reaching out she seized Elyn's hand her eyes beseeching as words tumbled from her mouth.

Elyn glanced helplessly at Alex who spoke soothingly to Leila, apparently convincing her that all was well, and that the fracas had nothing to do with her or her child. Relief lightened her face and she relaxed back on the couch.

Jehan came back with the inhaler, and her expression was one of acute concern. She drew Alex aside and murmured swiftly in Arabic. He replied briefly, asking her a question to which she nodded, then they rejoined Elyn at the examination table.

Twenty minutes later the Sheikha left the examination room on the arm of her maidservant, fully cloaked and veiled, with her baby lying in the correct position. Her brief but heartfelt thanks touched Elyn. She felt an affinity with the proud and independent young woman who did not easily reveal her thoughts and fears and who was prepared to fight for what she believed in. Her role as wife of the Tuareg chieftain would require her to accept responsibility for the wellbeing of her people in a way similar to that of Elyn with her patients.

'Any other problems out there?' Alex asked Jehan as she came in from the waiting room.

'No, Doctor. Now just the routine urine tests, blood pressures and iron injections.'

'Then we'll leave you to get on with it.' He turned to Elyn. 'You come with me.'

'But, I was just—' Elyn began.

'When will you learn not to argue,' Alex grated, and, grasping her arm above the elbow, he propelled her forcibly along the passage.

Pausing only to unlock the door, he pushed her into the small room where the clinic's drug supplies were kept, snapped the light on and shut the door behind them.

He swung Elyn round so that she stumbled backwards against him, but the sensation of his taut, muscular body against her back was dispelled by the ice in his voice. Gripping her shoulder he shook her hard.

'Look, straight ahead, what do you see?' His glacial tone—soft and deadly, sent ripples of fear down her spine.

Her eyes fastened on the dangerous drugs cupboard directly in front of her. As she realised the significance of the half-open door, the floor heaved beneath her feet.

There was a roaring in her head, like rushing water, and everything went black and she felt herself falling . . . falling . . .

She came round a few moments later to find herself slumped on the only chair with her head between her knees. Alex was bathing her face and neck with a handful of cool, wet tissues.

Acutely embarrassed, she immediately tried to sit up, but he held her head down. 'Wait,' he said crisply, 'Now, come up slowly. All right?'

'Mmm,' Elyn didn't dare nod, her head still felt like a balloon that might float away, on the slightest breath of wind. She clung to the chair and took several deep breaths while she waited for the room to stop swaying.

A glass beaker was pressed into her hand. 'Drink,' Alex ordered.

'What is it?' Elyn stared at the colourless liquid, her mind still cloudy.

'Look, I wouldn't have to resort to poison to get rid of you,' Alex retorted, 'it's water. Now drink it, you have work to do.'

Too confused and weary to argue, Elyn swallowed the water and felt slightly better.

'Work? In here?' She blinked up at him, 'But it's not time for the evening medication yet, surely?' She was unaware of the appealing vulnerability in her sapphire eyes, which seemed too large for her pale face, with its halo of damp curls.

She saw Alex's jaw tighten and a hardness come into his eyes as he repeated coldly, 'Yes, work. You will do a complete stock check of all drugs on the Poisons List and those covered by the Dangerous Drugs Act in that cupboard. When you have finished, bring the list to my office and we'll compare it with the current stock and withdrawal sheets, then we'll know exactly what and how much your friend Preston has stolen.'

'He's not—' Elyn began, then stopped, still barely comprehending the enormity of what had happened. Still unwilling to accept that Tim's friendship had been a hollow sham, that he had been pleasant to her, had flirted with her, only because she was a doctor and, as such, was a passport to the drugs he craved.

'He's not a thief? Is that what you were going to say? Jehan finds the cupboard open, the shelves rifled and disarranged. Preston tricks a young inexperienced nurse into handing over one of the only two sets of keys to the pharmacy door and cupboards. Your keys, which are still missing. If *he's* not a thief, where do you think that leaves you?' His tone was blistering.

Elyn flinched and tried to look away, but he seized her chin and forced her head up.

'Or were you going to say that he's not your friend.' Am I expected to believe that?' Alex threw at her. 'You insisted he was. You refused to listen to a word against him. When I tried, and I tried several times to warn you that he was an addict, you—'

'I didn't know,' Elyn murmured, 'I honestly didn't know. I thought—'

'You made it very clear what you thought,' Alex snarled. 'You thought I was being petty, you thought I wanted to interfere in your private life, your choice of friends.' His mouth was bitter as he snorted in disgust. 'For God's sake, what kind of doctor are you?'

The shaft hit deep and hard. Elyn's eyes closed and Alex dropped his hand from her chin in contempt. Feeling tears of shame prick her eyelids, Elyn looked down at her hands, still clasping the beaker. They were trembling as realisation of how she'd been used, tricked, filled her with anger, guilt and a torturing self-doubt. How could she have been so blind?

If she hadn't been so involved with her own problems, her own feelings for Alex, she might have realised that Alex's reaction to Tim had nothing at all to do with her, but was based on observation of certain clinical signs and behaviour patterns. It was her self-absorption that had been responsible for this. Her conceit in imagining that Alex would care one way or the other about her friendship with Tim. Alex had been concerned only because he saw that Tim was trying to gain a foothold in the clinic.

Black despair filled Elyn. With great deliberation she placed the beaker on the bench and slowly raised her head. But Alex had gone. She had been so deep in thought she had not heard him leave.

It made no difference. She knew what she had to do. She had no choice. He would never trust her again. There would always be doubt.

Besides could she ever again trust herself? It was part of a doctor's job not to allow personal matters to influence judgments. Yet her emotional problems had blinded her to the reality of Tim's condition.

What if such a thing had occurred in the clinic? What if she had missed some factor in another patient's illness or treatment?

Panic seized her and she leapt up from the chair, reaching for the door handle. But Alex had told her to remain here, to check the plundered drugs cupboard. If she suddenly appeared on the ward, heaven alone knew what he might do.

Biting her lip, she sat down again. Placing her hands flat on the work bench, she drew on all her reserves of will-power. She must be calm and concentrate on one thing at a time. First, the stock check, then, this evening, when Jehan had handed over to the night staff and Alex had gone off duty, she would come back.

Magda would think it a bit odd, but as Elyn would not require an assistant, it would not interfere too much with ward routine. She would double-check against her notes every patient she had dealt with.

Once that was done and she was absolutely certain nothing had been overlooked, she would go and see Alex. There was only one course left open to her, and that was to resign and leave the clinic.

With a sense of loss and desolation too deep for tears, Elyn pulled a note-pad and pencil towards her and opened wide the cupboard door.

'You surely aren't going back to the wards tonight?' Disapproval drew Maud's brows together in a deep frown. 'My dear girl, you can't go on like this. You only picked at that lovely meal Nefra left for us, and there's scarcely enough meat on your bones as it is. You've got shadows under your eyes any panda would be proud of, and now you're going back to do even more work. You're going to make yourself ill.' Maud folded her arms across her patterned silk bosom and drummed her fingers against the soft, bulging flesh of her upper arm.

'I don't know what Alex is thinking of, expecting you to work those hours. I've only had Henry to look after and my legs and feet are killing me.' Her voice softened and she smiled. 'Mind you, it's worth every twinge. He's so much better already.'

'I am so glad, Maud,' Elyn said sincerely. 'We're very pleased with his progress. It's not just the drugs that are speeding up his recovery, it's the quality of the nursing.'

Maud's eyes crinkled at the corners. 'Well, he's all I've got. I've got to look after him,' she said simply.

Elyn pulled a thick cardigan over her tunic top. 'It wasn't Alex's idea that I go back. He doesn't know.' She kept her voice light. 'It's some work I want to do for myself.'

'What, like research, you mean?' Maud's frown faded as interest took its place.

'Sort of,' Elyn agreed evasively. 'I'd better go, Maud. I've a lot to do and I'd like to get to bed before midnight.'

'Just don't overdo it,' Maud warned. 'I know work is supposed to keep your mind off—other things,' she paused significantly, 'but if you get too run down, you'll be ill, and that won't be much help to anyone.' She sighed gustily. 'I sometimes think Alex Davidson is the biggest fool I know.' She flashed a guilty glance at Elyn, who blinked in surprise at Maud's uncharacteristic criticism. 'Don't you tell him I said so.'

'I wouldn't dream of it,' Elyn assured her, in all honesty.

Maud fiddled with the ends of her dressing-gown sash. 'I wish—' she began explosively, then sighed once more. 'I suppose he has his reasons, but I must say they don't make much sense to me.'

She grinned at Elyn, her irritation dissolving as quickly as it had flared. 'Don't mind me, dear, I'm just rambling. I expect I'll be in bed when you get back, so I'll see you in the morning.'

Elyn gave her a brief smile, curious as to what was on Maud's mind. She seemed torn between saying and not saying something concerning Alex.

Elyn shrugged mentally. She had enough pressing problems of her own without becoming involved with other peoples'. Besides, it really wasn't any of her business.

She let herself out of the bungalow and paused for a moment on the doorstep, looking up at the sky. The evening air was cold, as it always was, but tonight there was something different about it. It did not have its usual crispness, that invigorating edge like chilled, sparkling wine, so welcome after the day's heat.

Tonight the air was heavy, almost thick. Another sandstorm?

Elyn did not think so, there was no dust on the breeze. In fact there was no breeze at all. The air was absolutely still. Even the palm trees had ceased their whispering. A brooding, almost menacing silence crouched over the compound.

As her eyes searched the inky blackness above her, something else struck Elyn. There were no stars. Usually the black velvet sky was pierced with a million coldly twinkling points of light, but tonight not one single star was visible.

Elyn shivered, not simply from the cold. Then, far in the distance, a jagged flash split the sky. It was followed by a growling rumble, so soft that Elyn felt rather than heard it.

Of course, a thunderstorm. It must be cloud blotting out the stars. Elyn chided herself for her fanciful notions. She was tired and her nerves were too tightly strung. Maud was right. She should try and get more rest. Well, she'd be getting enough of that once she left the clinic and returned to England.

Clamping down hard on her thoughts before the pain became unbearable, Elyn set off quickly but quietly across the compound. The freak weather conditions were driven from her mind by more immediate concerns.

As she passed Alex's bungalow she felt a stirring of relief at the light glowing through the drawn curtains. He was safely at home and unless an emergency recalled him to the clinic, they were unlikely to see one another again that night until she had completed her self-imposed task and was ready to face him.

Entering the back door of the clinic, Elyn recalled the scene in Alex's office when she had taken him the completed drug stock-list.

She had expected anger, a scathing indictment of her carelessness, stupidity and irresponsibility, and had mentally prepared herself for it. Instead, he had seemed preoccupied, as if wrestling with a problem even more important and demanding. He had looked up from his paperwork, taken the list she proffered, and scanned it quickly. Then telling her to read it aloud he had checked the other two sheets, making notes as he did so. The whole business had taken only a few minutes.

'So,' Alex looked across the desk to where Elyn stood, 'now we know exactly what's missing.' He glanced at his notepad, 'Several brands of barbiturates, all high-potency, and a quantity of narcotic-based analgesics, tablets and ampoules.'

Elyn remembered something. Though hating to say it, she knew she had no choice, it had to be faced. 'He must also have taken the Omnopon and syringe that Jehan left in the nurses' cubicle for Ali yesterday afternoon, just after we brought Henry in.'

Alex nodded briefly. 'I guessed that, though it didn't dawn until Jehan reported the unlocked cupboard. I assumed, as you obviously had, that she had not had time to go to the pharmacy, so I used the standby ampoule from the ward drugs box for Ali.'

He shuffled the sheets together, tapping them into neatness on the desk top. 'Preston knew exactly what he wanted. He knew enough about pharmaceutical data to take only the strongest. You know what that means?'

Elyn nodded reluctantly. 'He's a confirmed addict.' She shrugged helplessly, 'But I don't remember seeing any puncture marks on his arms.'

'He's probably injecting into his thighs. Europeans working in this climate usually wear short-sleeved shirts, and sometimes even strip to the waist. He's not too far gone to realise that needle marks would betray him.' Alex tipped back his chair, frowning. 'If he'd not been in such a hurry, leaving the shelves in disorder and the cupboard door unlocked, we might not have missed the drugs for several days.'

'I don't understand why the—theft wasn't discovered last night,' Elyn said tentatively.

'Because after Jehan had gone to the pharmacy to get

the Omnopon for Ali, no-one had reason to go again until I sent Jehan for the inhaler. I had prepared the evening medication and stocked the ward drug boxes at the same time as the antimony injections for the bilharzia admissions.'

Elyn swallowed. 'What are you going to do?'

'About Preston?' Alex tapped his teeth with his pen. 'I've no choice. I shall have to notify the police.' Though apparently abstracted, he was in fact watching Elyn closely.

Elyn glanced down, 'What will they do to him?' she asked in a low voice.

It was through Tim that she was having to give up the job that meant everything to her, forcing her to leave the place which, despite its handicaps and discomforts, she had grown to love, even as she loved the steel-eyed man on the other side of the desk.

Yet she pitied Tim Preston. He was destroying himself, committing slow, ugly suicide.

Alex shook his head. 'It depends. If he's a pusher too, and he'd probably have to be to support his habit, after all,' he said drily, 'he couldn't count on a lucky break like this every day.' Embarrassment flamed Elyn's face and she looked away quickly as Alex concluded, 'It could mean a very long jail sentence.'

Despite the stifling heat, Elyn shivered. Prisons out here were far more primitive than those in England. It was not unheard of for a man to be locked away and literally forgotten. Yet if Tim was selling drugs on the black market he was guilty of a terrible crime. He was peddling death.

Alex's voice broke into her thoughts. 'Right,' he said briskly, 'you've missed your lunch break, so you'd better grab something to eat, then get back on the wards.'

Elyn's head jerked up. This wasn't at all what she had expected. Where was the rocket? Why didn't he get it over with, tell her she had let him down, had proved unworthy of the job.

'Well?' he snapped.

'But—I thought—'

'But what?' he barked, 'surely there's work waiting for you?'

'Yes—it wasn't that—' Elyn began in confusion.

'Then whatever else it is will keep.' Alex deliberately cut her off, and, pulling his chair forward, bent his dark head and resumed his paperwork.

She was dismissed. Elyn knew that if she spoke he would not answer. He would not even hear. He had developed the art of directing his whole attention to whatever task he had in hand.

Realising protest was useless and would only irritate him, and deep down secretly glad of a few hour's respite from both the telling off she was sure would be forthcoming, and the dreaded moment of actually informing him she was leaving, Elyn quietly left the office.

After a snatched lunch with Maud, who was bubbling over with high-spirits at Henry's continued progress, Elyn returned to the wards. She had used every spare moment not actively engaged with new patients to re-examine those now progressing towards recovery, trying to reassure herself that her ignorance of Tim's condition had been a fluke, the only flaw in an otherwise perfect record.

When it was time for the afternoon ward round, her painstaking thoroughness was not lost on either Jehan or Alex.

The Chief Nurse's forehead puckered in a mildly puzzled frown, as she glanced several times at her watch, while Alex stood slightly to one side, seeming in Elyn's fevered imagination to be distancing himself from her, as if her oversight had made her something to be avoided at all costs.

Jehan checked the time yet again and stepped forward to speak to Elyn, but Alex stopped her with a sharp frown and a brief shake of his head. Jehan shrugged imperceptibly and Elyn, totally unaware of the silent exchange, was also oblivious to the self-mockery on his face or the tenderness of his gaze.

Thunder growled once more as Elyn entered the office. The deep rolling echo seemed to vibrate upwards through her feet. She paused for a moment, uneasy, but not knowing why.

Thunderstorms had never bothered her before, even as a child. In fact it had been Aunt Connie who had sat bolt upright in a chair in the centre of the room as far from every metal or electrical object as she could get, while Elyn pulled back the curtains, gazing entranced at what she called nature's firework display.

She shook her head and sighed. She was being over imaginative, and silly. The sooner she was immersed in the task she had set herself, the better.

During the next two hours Elyn worked intently. Though most of the time hunched over the desk, she did make a couple of trips onto the wards, to confirm the dosage of a particular drug and to double-check a lab-report against the Kardex.

The thunder continued to rumble, trapped in the valley. Several times the lights flickered as lightning raked the sky, its cold incandescence momentarily brighter than the artificial light. But Elyn ignored it, concentrating on her work.

Then the job was complete. She had finished. Her relief at the knowledge that her oversight had been an isolated lapse brought no comfort. That single instance was one too many. Alex had warned on her arrival that his standards were high. His doubts about her ability to adhere to them had been only too plain. Now, her naivety and reluctance to face facts had confirmed them.

One thing bewildered her. She could not understand why he had not taken the opportunity to sack her at once. When she had taken the list to the office she had expected him to say something, had mentally braced herself. Why hadn't he? His behaviour was incomprehensible.

He could not possibly ignore what had happened. His position and responsibility as Director of the clinic put that out of the question, apart the fact that the police were to be involved. Why was he prolonging her agony? Why couldn't he just get it over with?

Perhaps he was waiting for her to make the first move. That must be it. Though arrogant and impatient he was neither petty nor spiteful. He must be waiting for her to offer her resignation, which of course he would accept, but which would allow her to retain a little pride. Elyn bit her lip. There was no further reason for delay. He had only limited patience and she must have already used up most of it. Though it would make no difference, at least she could tell him with certainty there was no other case in which she had been remiss.

How unimportant even that was compared with the fact that she was about to turn her back on everything she had ever wanted, a job she adored in a country which fascinated her. But even more devastating, she would never again see the man she loved.

Alex Davidson had become part of the very fabric of her existence. He was her employer, her colleague. Working with him had been incredibly demanding, yet had drawn from her responses of skill and endurance she had not known she possessed. She had learned more about the practice of medicine in the few weeks she had been at Khalifa, than in the four years since she had left Medical School.

He was arrogant and dictatorial, yet he never demanded more from his staff than he himself was prepared to give, and she loved him. She loved him so much it hurt.

For a moment Elyn tried to convince herself she would be happy to remain at the clinic under any circumstances, simply to be where he was. To work with him would be enough. She would bury her desires and her emotions, crushing them down into some deep secret place in her heart where they would remain until either they died or she did.

But she knew it was a lie. She could not live like that. She was not strong enough. Sooner or later she would betray herself, and when that happened Alex's contempt would in any case make it impossible for her to remain at the clinic.

So maybe it was all for the best. She would return to England and get another hospital job, and relegate her time in Egypt to the status of a dream, a bitter-sweet memory which, if God was merciful, would fade in time.

Elyn pushed her chair and stood up. She must see Alex now, get it over with while she had the strength and determination to handle the painful interview with dignity.

Replacing all the files and glancing round to ensure she had left the office as she found it, Elyn closed the door behind her and walked quickly down the passage to the back door.

As she opened it, the storm broke with terrifying ferocity. Lightning split the sky on all sides, forking to earth in a series of brilliant flashes. Simultaneously, thunder crashed with a noise that hurt her ears.

This was unlike any other storm Elyn had experienced. An uncontrolled power seemed to have taken over the skies, mocking human beings and their puny efforts to harness the forces of nature with dams and wells and irrigation schemes.

There was a strange smell in the air, air which crackled with electricity generated by the elements at war overhead. Elyn hesitated, shaken by the violence of the storm and the sheer volume of sound.

Gritting her teeth, she stepped out into the compound, feeling infinitely small and vulnerable. Though Alex's house was only yards away, by the time she reached it her heart was pounding unevenly and her teeth chattered.

She hammered on his door, desperate to get the next few minutes over with so that she could hurry back to her own bungalow and the simple comforts of a cup of tea, a warm shower and a good night's sleep.

She had raised her hand to knock a second time when the door opened and Alex's tall figure stood silhouetted against the softly-lit hallway.

Another jagged spear of lightning illuminated Elyn's pale face and she winced as a tremendous thunderclap drowned her rehearsed greeting.

Alex leaned forward and drew her inside, closing the door on the storm's violence. But the turbulence within Elyn's breast only increased as Alex looked down at her, his face bland and his eyes shadowed.

Part of Elyn's mind registered his green and white checked shirt, the rolled-up sleeves exposing his deeply tanned arms, his green cord trousers and loafers. His freshly combed hair was still damp from the shower.

'Yes Elyn? What can I do for you?' His voice was deep and quiet and totally devoid of inflection.

Elyn struggled with the urge to turn and run.

'I take it you haven't come because you're afraid of the storm?' he enquired with a sardonic lift of his brows.

That gave Elyn the courage she needed. Tilting her chin she clasped her hands in front of her and, moistening dry lips, she met his gaze.

'No, I've come—' she swallowed, 'I've come to tell you I'm leaving the clinic. I will let you have my resignation in writing tomorrow.'

She had done it. It was out. She had been polite, dignified, and straight to the point. All that needed to be worked out was the terms of her notice and that would be done tomorrow.

Then, her momentary pride in her achievement was shattered as realisation struck. It was over, finished. Now there was no going back.

'You had better come in for a moment,' Alex said calmly, stretching out a hand to guide her into the sitting room.

'No,' Elyn said sharply, 'thank you.' She moved quickly out of reach. He mustn't touch her. She wouldn't be able to cope if he touched her. 'I've said what I came to say. There's nothing more to discuss. I did try to tell you this afternoon, but—' she broke off, turning to the door.

She heard a movement and sensed he was right behind

her. Don't let him touch me, she prayed.

As if she had spoken aloud he came no closer.

'I refuse to accept it,' he said quietly.

Elyn froze. She couldn't have heard him properly. Or he must have misheard her. Not daring to look round, she cleared her throat, trying to steady her voice.

'Please don't tease,' she spoke through trembling lips. 'It wasn't easy, though I'm aware I had little choice. If it's notice you're concerned about, naturally I'll stay until you find a replacement,' she finished wildly, clutching the door handle for support.

'I never joke about serious matters,' Alex retorted. 'I refuse to accept your resignation,' he repeated flatly. 'You have a contract, I insist you honour it.'

Elyn's head spun. Nothing made sense. She had worked it out. Logic dictated she must leave, now he had overturned all her painful reasoning. With just one sentence he had plunged her into total confusion. It was too much. She couldn't take any more.

Elyn wrenched open the door, only to find her way barred by Alex's arm and a sheet of water.

The clouds had begun to shed their burden. Rain was falling in torrents. Hurled from the sky it drummed on the roofs, hissed against the windows. It bounded off the parched sandy ground which, even as they watched, stunned and speechless, softened then liquified, forming puddles then pools, until it seemed that the house and the other nearby buildings were floating on a vast muddy lake.

Wide-eyed, Elyn looked up at the man beside her. His arm went round her shoulders and tightened, but the movement was completely unconscious. His face as he stared out at the deluge was dark and grim.

'Oh my God,' he whispered.

CHAPTER EIGHT

'QUICKLY,' Alex ordered, pulling Elyn round to face him. 'Go and fetch Maud. If she's asleep, wake her. We're going to need every pair of hands.'

Events were moving too fast for Elyn. 'What for?' she asked dazedly.

'If this rain lasts any length of time, Khalifa could be destroyed,' Alex replied grimly. 'Look at the surface water here in the compound. The wadis will already be filling with water running off the hillsides. There's no outfall in the valley and it can't soak away fast enough. The oasis is the lowest point.'

'A flash flood?' Elyn gasped in horror. Now she recognised the reason for her unease. Tim had mentioned the rare phenomenon when they had discussed climate and conditions on the journey from Cairo.

Alex nodded. 'We'll be needed in the oasis. Your first priority is to get everyone out of their houses and onto higher ground. You must organise shelter and hot food, then set up an Aid Station to deal with those needing medical attention.'

'But, why me?' Elyn began, 'I've never—'

'Who else, for God's sake?' Alex shook her. 'You're a doctor. You've been trained to handle emergencies. Leave a competent skeleton staff to cover the clinic. Take the rest of the nurses and fix up some sort of refuge for the women and children.'

He paused for a moment, his thoughts obviously racing ahead to envisage every possibility.

'I'll radio Kharga, see if they've been hit and ask for whatever help they can send. Then Salah and I will organise the men into teams to reinforce and divert the irrigation channels. We might be able to contain the

172

water and avoid widespread flooding.'

He looked down at her, taut and decisive. 'Mohammed will bring the ambulance back to collect you and the nurses. You instruct him from then on.'

Elyn's courage failed her. He expected too much. He was so strong, so capable, carrying responsibility as unconsciously as breathing.

She had never before faced a situation like this. She wasn't sure she could cope with it. She looked up at him, pale and nervous. 'I'm—I'm not—'

Alex drew her closer, his hands gripping her upper arms. The firm grasp infused warmth into her shaking body. His eyes, as green and hard as jade, gleamed like a cat's.

'Woman, I need you,' he said harshly.

The moment was timeless, then Elyn felt her strength returning. Her limbs ceased trembling and her back stiffened.

Never had she dreamed of hearing those words from him. He needed her. Regardless of what happened tomorrow, and she was still too confused by his refusal to accept her resignation even to begin to comprehend his reasons, tonight he needed her. She would not let him down.

'What about the clinic? Is there any danger of flooding here?' Elyn felt the adrenalin pouring into her veins, giving her body strength and purpose, sharpening her mind for the challenge that faced them.

'We're on a slight rise,' Alex replied quickly, slipping a casual arm around her as he pointed across the compound. 'There are drainage channels on both sides funnelling into the old river bed. We should be all right.'

Elyn frowned as she thought quickly. 'The safest place in the oasis is the new school. It's only a shell, but the roof is complete and sound, and it is the largest building as well as being up on the hillside.'

Alex nodded. 'That will do fine. There's a fissure in the rocks to the left of the building which should channel all the water away. But the access is only a rough path, so watch your step.' He reached into his trouser pocket.

'Here are my keys,' he handed them to her. 'Take what you need from the pharmacy to cope with general first-aid. Have any serious injuries brought up here. Tell the nurses to fetch extra blankets from the linen store, then open up the kitchen and get some hot soup prepared and sent up to the school.' He added an afterthought, 'And get some waterproof sheets.'

'Waterproof sheets?' Elyn repeated blankly.

'We don't often need oilskins or plastic macs in the desert,' Alex reminded her with grim humour, 'you'll be outside quite a bit and without some protection you'll be soaked and chilled in seconds. Cut a hole for your head and tie something round your waist. It's hardly adequate, but it's the best we can do.'

Elyn peered out into the darkness. The rain showed no sign of ceasing and had settled into a relentless downpour. 'I'll need oil-lamps, lots of them,' she said.

Alex nodded. 'Take whatever you need from the clinic.'

'Right, I'm on my way.'

Suddenly Alex pulled her against him. Turning her face up he kissed her hard on the mouth. 'Be careful,' he growled. 'Now get moving.'

Elyn was splashing and squelching through the liquid mud to her bungalow before she realised fully what had happened. But there was no time to wonder. Too much depended on her keeping her mind firmly on the task ahead.

Within half an hour Elyn had her team organised.

'I'll see to the soup, dear,' Maud volunteered as she struggled blearily into trousers, shirt and two cardigans. 'Leave the youngest nurse with me, she'll only be a hindrance to you. If you see Nefra and she's not tied up with her family, ask her to come up here. We'll bring the first batch of soup, bread and coffee to the school within an hour in my Land Rover, and I'll send some over to the clinic for the staff and any injured.'

Elyn breathed a sigh of relief, Maud was magnificent.

Next Elyn darted across to the nurses' block for Jehan. She was already dressed and, having seen the force of the rain, had anticipated the situation and was waking the other nurses as Elyn burst in.

As the nurses emerged, tired after a day's duty, but alert and anxious to help, Elyn sent them for lamps and spare oil, blankets and waterproof sheets, with instructions to meet in Alex's office.

She and Jehan hurried to the pharmacy. While the Chief Nurse made up first-aid packs, Elyn checked her bag, adding to her stock of cotton wool and bandages, pain-killing drugs, disposable syringes, her stethoscope, the sphyg. and other items which would be required in the event of a major accident.

As they returned laden to the office, Elyn heard the ambulance containing Alex and the two paramedics roar out of the compound.

By the time Elyn had explained the plan to the nurses, and they had all shrouded themselves in the thin rubber sheets and covered their heads with squares of the same material, Mohammed had returned.

'Is very bad, *hanem*,' he grimaced in reply to Elyn's question. 'People run around, scream and shout, not know where to go. Try to save their animals and possessions. Houses fall down as water make mud bricks crumble.'

Elyn felt the blood drain from her face. How could Alex expect her to cope with it all? She swallowed as the nurses murmured among themselves. Then as one, they looked at her, waiting for her instructions.

'Right,' Elyn said calmly, betraying none of the apprehension that clawed at her stomach, 'Magda will remain here in the clinic with one nurse and two pupils.' She addressed the senior night nurse. 'I leave it to your discretion to give sedatives where necessary. This storm will have disturbed quite a few of the patients. Reassure them we're doing all we can for their families. I'll write up any sedation when I get back.' Heaven alone knows when that will be, she added silently.

'Jehan, Moni and the two trainees, you come with me.'

They loaded the ambulance, climbed in and set off down the track.

Sitting next to Mohammed, Elyn could hardly see through the windscreen. The wipers laboured under the volune of water pouring from the skies. Intermittent lightning streaked earthward, followed by thunderclaps which rolled and echoed around the valley. It seemed to Elyn as if the storm was moving away. Surely it couldn't last much longer. But it still rained.

Elyn could hear the sound of water even above the engine. It drummed on the ambulance roof, gurgling muddily down the track, rolling small pebbles and stones along with it. It gushed and spouted from fissures in the sloping valley sides, roaring down to the wadi in a thousand fast-moving streams, transforming the dry, dusty riverbed into a raging cataract.

'Did Dr Davidson get through on the radio?' Elyn asked hopefully.

Mohammed shook his head. 'No, *hanem*, too much electrical interference from the storm.'

That meant they were on their own. They would have to do whatever needed to be done alone.

'Did he say where he would be?' Elyn asked, as much to take her mind off the frightening scene outside as to know where Alex could be found should she be faced with something she couldn't handle.

'He by well-head. He make men in two groups, one to move animals and food stores, other to open irrigation ditches, then build bank and dig trenches to divert water down old river bed to low land.'

Elyn nodded. She could picture Alex, the rain plastering his dark hair to his skull, and pouring down his lean face as he shouted directions and encouragement to the men with him. For Elyn knew he would be in the ditches with them, moving mud and stone with his bare hands, the hands of a gifted surgeon. He would blister them on a pick or shovel, doing the work of two, rather than see the oasis drown.

They entered the village and the first signs of devastation became visible in the headlights. A small house, built at the foot of a gully, had been reduced to a pile of muddy rubble. Dark waters still foamed about the ruin. The body of a drowned goat was wedged against two palm trees, themselves uprooted by the torrent, which had erupted from the hillside without warning.

Elyn shuddered. This night would remain etched on her memory for as long as she lived.

'Stop here, Mohammed,' Elyn ordered as they entered the cluster of houses and the market place which were the heart of Khalifa.

The scene was one of pandemonium. Women, old and young, splashed about clutching terrified children, and armfuls of household goods. Shrieks and wails rose above the pounding rain.

One old woman, her black sodden robes clinging to her bent body, collided with the ambulance. Her eyes were wide and staring and her mouth gaped in a soundless scream. She staggered and stumbled away in the darkness, clasping two squawking hens.

'That her house we passed,' Mohammed said tersely.

Elyn leapt out and ran to open the back door. 'Jehan, tell them about the school. Make them understand they'll be dry and safe there. They must leave their houses now. Tell them to bring lamps, dry clothing and a cup or bowl, but nothing else. Mohammed and I will unload the ambulance then I'll send him back here to pick up those who can't walk.'

Jehan nodded and, followed by the nurses, jumped down into the swirling, muddy water.

Elyn scrambled back into her seat and they drove as fast as the dangerous conditions permitted to the school.

While Elyn lit the lamps, hanging one either side of the door as a homing beacon for the drenched and frightened villagers, Mohammed unloaded the blankets and boxes

'We'd better put First-Aid at the top of the room,' Elyn decided, 'then those needing medical attention won't block the doorway.' She pulled off her makeshift mac and scarf and rolled them up beside her bag.

'There are boards here, *hanem*,' Mohammed called. 'We make tables, one for First-Aid and one for food.'

'Set them up one either side,' Elyn shouted. 'Have you anything we could make some signs with? It might help the villagers when they come in.'

Mohammed produced a pillowcase which he tore in half, and Elyn rummaging in her tunic pockets, found her only lipstick. With a little sigh she handed it to the paramedic who scrawled in Arabic over the white cotton. Then, handing the flattened stub back to Elyn with a rueful grin, he hurried away to hang up the signs, then out to the ambulance and back into the oasis.

A few minutes later the women and children began arriving, accompanied by the nurses.

Soon the large room rang with chattering, crying voices. Jehan moved among them, looking for signs of serious shock, directing those with minor injuries to Elyn, soothing and calming, helping the very old and very young into dry clothing and the comforting warmth of the blankets.

Elyn was kept busy, cleaning and bandaging cuts and bruises. Mohammed returned with several old, bedridden patients and went back for others. One of the nurses set up a spirit-stove and was boiling kettlefuls of water while another tried to organise the casualties into an orderly line and move them away down the room once they'd been treated.

The volume of noise suddenly rose and Elyn glanced up the see Maud edging her way through the crush with two huge covered jugs. The girl following her carried a large tray of flat pitta bread. Mohammed brought up the rear with an emaciated old man in his arms.

'Nurse,' Elyn called sharply, 'leave what you're doing

and take over from Mohammed. Mohammed, can you clear the way for Maud, if they don't move back, some-one will get scalded.'

Mohammed eased the old man onto the floor where the nurse wrapped him in a blanket, then pushed his way through the clamouring women, shouting and gesturing, sending the women scuttling out of the way to let Maud through.

'Thanks, dear,' Maud beamed, her rosy face stream-ing water, which dripped onto the wet, shining rubber enveloping her, and formed a puddle on the floor.

She rested the jugs on the rough table and flexed her shoulders. 'There's hot coffee in the Land Rover,' she called to Mohammed, who waved an acknowledgement and went to get it.

'That little trainee can stay here and help serve, Nefra is up at the kitchen,' Maud bawled at Elyn over the noise. 'The next batch is almost ready. You're wanted down in the village.'

Elyn's head snapped up. She quickly finished tying the bandage around the arm of a doe-eyed girl of ten, and, giving her a quick smile, sent her back to her fretful mother.

'What's happened?'

'Accident out by the well-head. A house has collapsed and a man is trapped.'

Elyn's heart stopped. Alex was working by the well-head. Why had they sent for her if he was already there? It could only mean—she could not finish the thought, refused to admit the possibility. She began to pray, harder, more fervently than she had ever prayed. Don't let it be him. Please God, Alex must not be hurt.

Elyn scanned the crowed. 'Jehan,' she shouted and when the Chief Nurse looked up from the old woman she was comforting, Elyn beckoned to her.

'Moni,' Elyn turned to the nurse assisting her, 'you take over here. I think we've dealt with the worst of them.'

Jehan reached the table. '   s, *hanem*?'

'Get wrapped up again,' Elyn ordered quickly, 'there's been an accident and someone's trapped out by the well-head,' Elyn was already pulling the length of clammy rubber over her head. Knotting a bandage round her waist to keep it from flapping, she threw her instruments into her bag and snapped it shut.

Jehan had donned her sheet and seized a couple of first-aid packs from under the table as Elyn hurried to the door.

'I'll drop you off on my way back to the clinic,' Maud puffed as she caught up with them. 'Or do you want me to wait, in case—'

Elyn shook her head. 'No, Mohammed can bring the ambulance down when we need it. I'll send a boy for him. You'd better get the rest of that soup down to the men as quickly as you can. They'll be needing something hot.'

The rain lashed down, drenching Elyn in seconds, despite the waterproof, as she scrambled down the rough path to the waiting Land Rover. But she was scarcely aware of the chill night air and the cold water trickling down her neck, soaking into her already damp clothing, as Maud urged the vehicle through the cascade that poured from the gully at the side of the building and across the track.

Twice the engine coughed and faltered and Elyn could barely contain her impatience. She clenched her teeth to stop herself crying out in frustration, knowing that Maud was doing the best she could in the treacherous conditions.

At last they reached the well-head. Elyn was out of the vehicle before it had stopped, splashing through the turgid water, heedless of her sudden canvas shoes and the cotton trousers that clung dripping and filthy to her cold legs.

Panting, she reached the cluster of gesticulating men standing outside the partially destroyed house.

'Who—?' she had to swallow to moisten her fear-dried throat, 'who is in there?'

The men stared blankly, then began jabbering in Arabic. Elyn was desperately trying to make herself understood when Jehan came hurrying up behind her.

Touching Elyn's shoulder, the Chief Nurse shouted for silence which, to Elyn's surprise, she immediately got, then rattled off several questions.

'The man who is trapped is his father,' Jehan translated, indicating a small wiry man with a premature ly-seamed face who, like the other two, was soaked and shivering.

Elyn felt almost sick with relief. 'What happened?' she asked.

'They were part of the group moving stock to higher ground when they saw the house collapse. They tried to get in, but more of the wall fell down and they were afraid the old man will be killed if they touch anything.'

'Where is Dr Davidson?' Elyn demanded.

The excited jabber erupted again and once more Jehan shouted above them, singling out another man to answer.

'My son go for him. They not come yet, but my son send boy who say he not talk to doctor. Two men fell in wadi when bank give way. They drown maybe. Men try to get them out. Doctor help them, he in river too.'

Elyn closed her mind to the stab of anxiety. Alex would cope. She must cling to that thought, ignoring all doubt and fears. She turned to Jehan.

'We'd better get on and do what we can. It may be some time before Dr Davidson can get here.'

Jehan held the lamp high, staring at the half-collapsed pile of palm rafters and mud-brick. '*Hanem*, is not safe,' she declared nervously.

A hoarse, pain-filled cry issued from the building, ending in a gargling cough.

White-faced, Elyn turned to the nurse. 'We can't just do nothing. He could be dead before Alex arrives.'

'You be dead too if house fall down,' Jehan retorted at once, her face creased with anxiety.

'Look it's got to be me,' Elyn said reasonably, 'not

only am I the doctor he'll need, I'm also the smallest and lightest here.' She was managing to hide the nerve-shredding fear that almost choked her at the thought of climbing into the crumbling house through the pile of rubble that had been one half of it.

'I should be able to get in without any more falling down,' she said with a confidence only partially felt.

'What you do when you get inside?' Jehan cried, 'you can't bring him out yourself.'

Another cry ripped the air and Elyn grasped her bag more tightly. 'Well, I can't leave him there to suffer and do nothing. I'm going in. If necessary I'll sedate him until I can get him free.'

Seeing Elyn's white-lipped determination, Jehan said no more. Instead she turned to the men, telling them to fetch extra lamps and to start carefully moving some of the fallen brick out of the way to allow Elyn easier access.

With infinite caution Elyn picked her way across the crumbling masonry. Holding the lamp in front of her she tried to avoid the shadowed pockets which were waiting to trap her and pitch her forward into disaster.

Here and there the rubble had fallen across broken rafters and even her light weight caused the wood to creak and more rubble to slip, showering fragments and dust onto her saturated head. Each time she froze, waiting for the inevitable. But it did not come.

So she would start moving again, inching forward, crouched almost double, fighting to keep her balance, hampered by the lamp in one hand and her bag in the other.

At last she was inside what remained of the downstairs room. Raising the lamp she looked around and caught sight of the body of an old man, half-covered with rubble.

Elyn inched her way forward, beneath a ceiling bowed and cracked, through which protruded jagged spikes of broken wood.

'*Hanem*, you all right? You find him?' Jehan's voice,

taut with anxiety, floated faintly through the opening.

'Yes,' Elyn yelled back, and flinched as she stepped into ankle-deep water. The level was rising inexorably as water poured through the gaping holes, unable to escape. She had to get the old man out before he drowned.

'Send someone for the ambulance. I'll need a stretcher. Be quick, Jehan, there's a lot of water in here.'

Roused by the sound of Elyn's voice, the old man groaned and coughed, his head falling forward into the muddy water.

Elyn set the lamp down and quickly examined the part of him that was visible. Apart from bruising and grazes on his face and some swellings on his head, which must have occurred when the ceiling and walls caved in, he seemed unharmed. But his legs were trapped.

A length of broken rafter half hidden beneath a mound of rubble, lay across his calves. The sunbaked brick was crumbling and liquifying as the rain poured in, transforming it into thick oozing mud which slithered into the dark water lapping against the old man's face.

Kneeling down, Elyn pulled the lamp nearer, propping it on some broken brick and opened her bag. Taking out scissors she cut the old man's soaked and filthy garment, exposing his thin arm.

Pain-filled eyes were raised to hers and she murmured soothingly in a mixture of English and Arabic as she quickly filled the syringe, inserted the needle and pressed home the plunger.

Within seconds the old man's eyes dulled and closed and his head lolled heavily in Elyn's supporting hands.

Resting his face on her bag to keep it clear of the water, Elyn turned to examine the fall that had trapped him.

Glancing quickly round the cramped space which was all that was left of the room, she could see nothing which would help her. She had to free his legs to get him out. But there was nothing on which to balance the broken rafter and if she disturbed the rubble even a fraction it might be sufficient to bring the rest of the wall crashing down to bury them both.

Elyn forced down momentary panic. She must think. To free the old man's legs she needed to prop up the rafter. But the only thing available was mudbrick which would dissolve if she put it in water, especially with any pressure on it.

She rubbed the back of her hand across her dripping face and felt the roughness of mud against her cheek. She wiped her hand on the thick rubber sheet.

Of course, the rubber sheet. She would wrap a couple of bricks in the rubber, that would keep them dry long enough for her to pull him free.

Easing the old man's head up, Elyn took her scissors from the bag, then, cutting the soggy bandage which had kept the sheet around her waist, she struggled out of it.

After cutting several strips, she staggered to her feet and cautiously lifted three whole bricks from near the top of the pile.

Swiftly she wrapped the bricks as tightly as she could, then dropping to her knees once more, she gradually lifted the protruding edge of broken rafter.

The rubble slipped, sending a small landslide splashing into the water. Elyn smothered a cry. Every instinct urged her to run, to escape from this dark hole. Her heart was racing and suffocating waves of fear surged through her. The walls were closing in, and the water level was rising.

Elyn bit her lip until she tasted blood. She must not scream. If she screamed, her thin thread of control would snap. She must concentrate, think only of what she was doing. She could not stop now.

With painful slowness she lifted the wood until it was just clear of the old man's legs. The weight of rubble on the rafter strained the muscles of her arms and shoulders unbearably.

Using one foot she eased the bricks under the rafter.

Sobbing from exertion and fear she manoeuvred one brick on top of the other two, then, hardly daring to breathe, ignoring the searing agony in her shoulders, she lowered the rafter onto the bricks and closed her eyes, waiting.

Nothing moved, nothing fell. Shakily Elyn crawled to the old man's head. Holding his head up with one hand, she pulled her bag away with the other, then, grasping him under the arms, dragged him clear.

Jehan's voice came again, urgent anxious. '*Hanem*? You all right? Mohammed here now, he bring stretcher in.'

'No,' Elyn shouted at once, her voice cracking. 'No, Jehan, no one is even to try, the whole lot could fall. I've got the old man free.'

As she spoke she ran her hands over his legs, gently moving his feet and ankles. 'He is cut and bruised, but nothing is broken. I've given him morphine and he's unconscious. Tell the smallest man to slide the stretcher in over the rubble, but warn him not to touch the sides or any overhang.'

'Yes, *hanem*,' came the faint reply.

Splashing and slipping in the muddy water, Elyn hauled the old man towards the gap.

She heard a slithering grating sound and almost screamed before she realised it was the stretcher being pushed in.

She managed to get the old man onto it, and, wrapping the blanket securely around him, she fastened the straps across his thin body as tightly as she could.

All too aware of the steadily rising water and the crumbling brick, she began to ease the stretcher back up the oozing mound.

'He's coming out,' she called.

'I see him,' Mohammed shouted back. 'To the left, *hanem*, to the left,' came the urgent cry.

Praying he meant her left, Elyn wrenched the stretcher sideways and a few moments later felt it pulled from the other end.

She sank down on the rubble, her breathing ragged, every muscle trembling uncontrollably from strain and reaction.

The sounds of shouting and argument reached her.

'Elyn, for God's sake, get out of there at once,' Alex's voice reached her clearly. He sounded coldly furious.

'I'm coming,' she called, her own voice hoarse with exhaustion. Then she remembered. 'Just a minute, my bag.' He'd never forgive her if she left it, full as it was of valuable drugs and equipment.

'Forget the bloody bag,' he bellowed. 'If you don't come out this instant, I'll come in and get you.'

'You can't,' Elyn protested weakly, overcome by an urge to laugh, realising dimly that exhaustion and reaction were taking their toll now the emergency was almost over, 'the house will fall down.'

She began crawling again, and faintly heard the ambulance roar away.

She reached the entrance to the hole, and saw Alex leaning forward to grab her hands. Soaked and mud splattered, white to the lips with raw anger, he looked terrifying. 'What the hell did you mean by going in there?'

Elyn flinched and her wet foot slipped off a brick. Lurching sideways, she automatically put out a hand to save herself and felt the wall give way as she touched it.

Something glanced off the side of her head and she felt herself snatched up. A roaring noise filled her head and as the lamps faded and the world spun, she suddenly realised it had stopped raining.

She opened her eyes and blinked in the dim lamplight. Then struggled upright in the single bed. This wasn't her room. Where was she? She pushed back the covers and was shocked to see she was naked.

'Feeling better now?' Alex asked calmly as he entered the room, rubbing his head with a towel. He had

obviously just come from the shower and was wearing a
white bathrobe that emphasised not only the blackness
of his hair and his rich mahogany skin, but also his height
and the width of his shoulders.

Elyn had never been more aware of him as a man.
Clutching the bedclothes to her bosom she wriggled
lower down the bed, the crimson flush lending a glow to
her whole body.

'The storm—the oasis—' she stammered.

'Everything is under control,' he replied, 'the water is
receding and though there's some damage, it's not as
bad as we feared. By the morning most people will be
able to return home. Maud and the nurses are managing
splendidly.'

There was a silence, then in embarrassment and confusion Elyn burst out, 'Who—? How long—? I mean—
how dare you,' she spluttered.

'How dare I what?' he returned sardonically, standing
beside the bed, the towel hanging loosely from his hand.
'Strip you?' His face hardened. 'I'm a doctor, remember? You were knocked unconscious as the wall
collapsed. Your clothes were torn, soaked and filthy.
Your hair was matted with dust and mud. You had
cuts and grazes which, though minor, were bleeding.
I had no intention of putting you into my bed in that
state.'

'Why am I in your bed at all?' Elyn blurted, and
immediately wished she hadn't.

'Because I have things to say to you,' Alex gritted,
'and I seem to have the devil's own job keeping you in
one place while I say them, not to mention the interrup-
tions.'

Elyn blushed even more deeply as she recalled Mike's
unexpected reappearance in her life.

'I can't stay here,' she cried, 'you can't make me.'

Alex's face darkened. 'You don't seem to realise—
you are lucky to be alive.' He flung the towel away from
him, and, sitting down on the edge of the bed, seized
Elyn's shoulders. He seemed to be in the grip of the

same anger which had so shaken her when she emerged from the rubble.

'What the hell did you mean by going in there?' he demanded. The lamp-light cast brooding shadows across his face, and his eyes glittered.

For an instant Elyn was frightened of him, of his anger, of his strength, then her own temper flared.

'You asked me earlier today what sort of doctor I was,' she retorted, 'well, I'm the kind that doesn't leave a trapped man to drown in a few inches of water.'

'You little fool,' Alex raged, 'you should have waited until I came.'

'It would have been too late,' Elyn threw at him. 'I only just managed to get to him in time. Was I supposed to just let him die?' Elyn tossed caution to the winds. He would never know what it had cost her to go in there, how she had almost been sick with fear.

'Did you expect the flood water to stop rising until you got there?' she shouted, 'in any case you are too big to have got through the gap.'

'You could have been killed,' he grated, his fingers digging into the soft flesh of her bare shoulders.

'So could you when you were in the river,' Elyn cried, 'I was doing my job, just as you were. No allowances, you said, well, I didn't ask for any.'

'I don't give a damn about the job,' Alex stormed in furious exasperation, 'for God's sake, woman, I might have lost *you*.'

As his words registered, Elyn stopped breathing. There was total silence, broken only by the slow drip of water from the eaves to the ground.

Elyn's eyes met Alex's and an invisible current leapt between them.

'I love you,' he growled. 'I've known it for weeks and fought it all the way. I couldn't believe you were real. Thoughtful, caring, conscientious and beautiful into the bargain! I kept waiting for the snag, looking for the catch. But tonight when I arrived and Jehan said you were inside that collapsing pile of rubble—' he broke off.

Releasing her shoulders, he cupped her face tenderly between his hands, gazing at her as if every feature were infinitely precious to him. 'When I think of what you must have gone through—'

Then suddenly he dropped his hands from her face with a frustrated sigh and ran them through his tousled hair, turning slightly away.

'Hell,' he groaned, 'I don't even know if you—God knows I'm a difficult so-and-so. I'm demanding, arrogant—you were right—' he looked down at his feet once more, uncharacteristically diffident, waiting.

'Oh, Alex,' Elyn whispered, still so shattered by his declaration she could hardly believe it. 'I love you, I've loved you, I think, since that first moment in Cairo airport. But I thought—you and Samina—'

Alex leaned forward, sliding his hand along her arm and gently, almost reverently, kissed her mouth, his lips warm and soft on hers.

'Samina was bait,' he explained softly. 'She was sent by her father to lure me to his clinic in Cairo. There was never anything between us, though she did use all her powers of persuasion. I am not so easily bought.' There was an edge of contempt to his tone.

'I saw you kissing her the night we went to Kharga for the drug supplies,' Elyn said in a small voice. How that memory hurt.

'What you saw was Samina kissing me,' Alex reproved gently. 'Do you think after what had happened between us that afternoon, I would willingly have kissed another woman?'

Eyes shining, Elyn reached up and touched Alex's face, now at last free to do all the things she had wanted to do for so long.

'Are you really sure, Alex?' she asked hesitantly, 'I'm—Maud told me a little about why you came out here,' Elyn paused, choosing her words carefully, anxious not to hurt him by arousing tragic memories, but needing to hear from his own lips that the past was truly over and finished with. Elyn knew that despite the fact she loved Alex with all her heart and soul, she could not bear to spend the rest of her life competing with a memory.

'My dearest,' he murmured, his deep voice a caress that sent delicious shivers down Elyn's spine as his hand gently smoothed the ruffled curls from her forehead. 'I have never loved anyone as I love you. What Maud did not tell you, because neither she nor anyone else but the person concerned knew, was that the night Fiona died, she had spent the evening with another man. The same man, I soon learned, with whom she had spent numerous other evenings.' Alex's voice hardened and his face was tight with distaste and self-mockery, though his hand, resting against Elyn's cheek as if for reassurance, remained gentle.

'I found out afterwards that while the status of being the fiancée of a reasonably well-known surgeon appealed to her, the time demanded by his work did not. She re-ignited an old flame, a young man of her own age, whose only purpose in life was devising more and more outlandish ways to dispose of the fortune left to him by various wealthy relatives. Fiona craved constant excitement and attention—' he shrugged.

'Oh Alex, I'm so sorry,' Elyn's eyes sparkled with unshed tears.

'If you must be sorry, be sorry for her, not for me,' Alex said quietly. 'She is dead. I am alive, and in love with a woman who is all things to me. A colleague to respect—'

'Alex, don't,' Elyn begged, looking away from him, 'I made such a terrible mistake over Tim.'

'Your first and only mistake,' he turned her face back to his with a gentle finger. 'Elyn, I watched you pay for that mistake. Your own conscience punished you unmercifully.'

Realisation dawned on Elyn. 'You knew. Is that why you refused to accept my resignation?'

He nodded. 'That was one reason.'

'What was the other?' Elyn grinned impishly up at him.

'You little witch,' he growled. 'You know well enough. I had no intention of letting you escape from me.' His eyes searched hers. 'Will you marry me, Elyn? Could you face a lifetime out here?'

Elyn returned his gaze with serenity, filled with a happiness she had not dreamed could exist.

'Yes, I'll marry you, Alex. As for staying in Khalifa, there's nowhere else on earth I'd rather be, so long as we're together.'

Alex leaned forward pressing her gently back against the soft pillows. His mouth came down on hers, gently, tenderly, in a kiss of such aching sweetness Elyn thought her heart would burst. Then his breathing quickened and as Elyn slid her arms around his neck she felt the bedclothes fall away. The length of his lean, muscular body was against hers and she gave herself up joyfully to the long-contained passion which enveloped them both, sweeping them to the heights of ecstasy.

Later the pearl rays of the rising sun pierced the dawn mist that filled the oasis. It changed the desert sky from lemon and primrose to turquoise and aquamarine.

It reached out to the white walls of the clinic, gilding them pale gold, and spilled its warming light through the window of Alex's house, where, wrapped protectively in his arms, Elyn slept.

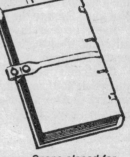